As Henry took in the sights and sounds around him, his chest started to tighten. Breathe. Slow. Even. Again. One more time. Now, think of something pleasant. The blonde from the coffee shop came to mind, a thought that had him shaking his head. Sure, she was pretty, but right now, he needed to find the woman who'd invited him to the social so she could introduce him to some of the people here. The job was his number one priority, and nothing else mattered, especially since *that job* was on the line.

He scanned the groups standing first, then the three long tables, his attention landing on the blonde coffee shop owner. *It figures she'd be here.* Next to her was the redhead. Were the two friends? Did it matter?

Henry swallowed hard and made his way toward Jenell, his step faltering when a tall man in black, with a head of curly dark hair, came to stand next to the blonde, leaning over to whisper something in her ear. Her lips parted, and she smiled, her reaction leaving a bad taste in Henry's mouth.

Who was this person? Her boyfriend? Husband? Henry hadn't noticed a ring on her finger.

The guy turned, and he saw the white collar. *The pastor.* But was he more than that to her? He seemed hands-on, touching her shoulder, but maybe he was that way toward everyone. Henry would keep an eye on him and watch them before he came to any conclusions. Not that it mattered either way.

Hidden in Plain City

by

Jerri Drennen

Redeeming the Reporter, Book 1

Hidden in Plain City

Cover Art by *Jennifer Greeff*

The Wild Rose Press, Inc.
PO Box 708
Adams Basin, NY 14410-0708
Visit us at www.thewildrosepress.com

Publishing History
First Edition, 2023
Trade Paperback ISBN 978-1-5092-5041-7
Digital ISBN 978-1-5092-5042-4

Redeeming the Reporter, Book 1
Published in the United States of America

Dedication

I want to dedicate this book to my late husband, Gary, who was not only my inspiration for the perfect love story we two shared but was the biggest supporter in my writing journey. He will forever be missed.

Chapter One

An ear-piercing boom resounded from behind the barbwire fence he stood next to, followed by a force so powerful, it threw him forward. He hit the ground hard, sharp rocks slicing deep into his hip. Dust and smoke cloaked the air and trapped stagnant breath in his lungs. Pain, so intense, radiated throughout the whole left side of his body. Convulsively, he swallowed, tasting a thick, metallic substance that made him gag. Agonizing wails off in the distance pulsated repeatedly like a rhythmic drumbeat. If he could, he'd cover his ears to block it out. Instead, he shuddered in a breath. The effort caused a gurgling to resonate in his throat. Time moved in unbearable slowness as he focused on something tangible, something to block out his misery. Above, sparse, fluffy clouds drifted between a sea of blue, seemingly so close he could reach out and touch them. "Hey, Mav...erick. Do you see what I see?" he choked out and wrenched his head sideways. That's when he saw his cameraman, the grotesque image shattering his soul into a million fractured pieces.

Henry Kiel jerked upright, wide awake, and gasping for air. His heart thudded so hard, it felt as if it would leave his chest.

That damn memory wouldn't quit, regardless of how many months had passed.

He shook his head to clear the fog and kicked the

covers from his legs, wiping perspiration from his upper lip. Henry didn't need the dream to remind him of what happened two and a half years ago. The constant ache in his hip and the guilt eating away at his soul accomplished that.

But why today of all days—his first on the job at the *Tribune*? It encompassed him like a bad omen. Whatever the reason, he couldn't let this shake him since it was his fresh start in a town so unlike any he'd ever lived before.

He threaded his hands through his mussed hair, then stumbled off to the shower.

Two-hundred and forty-three days clean and sober.

Time to tamp down his triggers and go forward. As long as he didn't make the same mistakes, he could get through this and stage a comeback. But as he'd learned in *'New Beginnings,'* taking one day at a time was the only way to remain in recovery.

There was no more dressing the part of an award-winning journalist. Those days were over. According to his editor, he was to look like everyone else in town. Simple. Jeans. Plain white shirt. Boots, or sneakers, which ever worked best for the day. Shaving appeared to be optional from what he'd seen, a plus since he was two weeks into growing a beard.

Thirty minutes later, he stepped out the door, almost tripping over the newspaper on the sidewalk. He picked it up, untucked it from the rubber band that held it together, and read the headline. *New Dairy Freeze opens on Fredrick Street.* Excitement abounded. How was he ever going to find fulfillment in writing about things like that?

He blew out a ragged breath, opened his car door, and slid behind the wheel. He was going to have to make this work because it was his only option until he redeemed himself in the eyes of news media.

While driving, he had to admire the quiet serenity of the neighborhood he now lived in. Two-story homes seemed to be the norm in Plain City, Arkansas. Most painted muted hues. Some brick. All with an array of different colored shutters and flower boxes. The lawns were manicured to a half an inch in height, and black torchlights lined the walkways. Typical Norman Rockwell, small town America, ideal for anyone raising a family. But a wife and kids had never been in Henry's plans. Hell, the longest relationship he'd had was a snowed-in week at the Alps, with twin sisters who insisted they did everything together.

He grimaced and shook the memory. Not one of his sober moments.

Being here in this quiet, uneventful town was like living on a different planet after the last ten years of his life. He'd traveled exclusively, to war-torn countries where gunfire was an everyday event. The constant action had charged his adrenalin and fueled his need for danger, a demand to go anywhere for a story. No matter the cost. And that had cost everything but his life.

This new normal was the opposite. Last evening, he'd been tortured by the sound of crickets chirping and tree frogs croaking. When one would stop, another would begin. *All night long with nothing to relieve the monotony.* He'd tossed and turned until he had stuffed a pillow over his head to block out the irritating noise. Somehow, he needed to get used to this new normal or buy a good pair of earplugs.

Minutes into his commute, he pulled into a parking spot in front of Allen's Coffee Shop. On the large picture window of the storefront, chalked outlines of steaming cups of coffee and cake donuts were drawn. In a big city, that would have been amateurish. Here, he guessed it was acceptable.

He hefted himself out of his Camry. He needed a cup of strong, black coffee and Simon Ridge, his new editor, said Allen's made the best in town.

As he stepped inside, a blend of aromatic coffee beans, cinnamon, and baked goods caused his mouth to water.

With a cynical eye, he glanced around. The interior had stainless steel bakery cases and retro type tables and chairs. The walls were a soothing light green with pieces of watercolor artwork displayed, instantly easing his troubled thoughts. Henry's stomach chose that moment to kick up a ruckus and growl like he hadn't eaten in a week. Not surprising since his appetite had gained ground with his stint in rehab.

When he glanced back at the counter, the few people waiting in line had turned to stare.

He cleared his throat and gave them a halfhearted smile. Their scrutiny was not unexpected since he was new to town and had fallen from grace.

"Good morning." He couldn't afford to start off on the wrong foot with anyone here. Not when he'd be interacting with most in some capacity.

"Next," a singsong voice said, drawing him to the person behind the counter. His jaw would have dropped had he not seen his share of gorgeous women in the world. They were plentiful in exotic ports of call. But this one had the greenest eyes he'd ever seen, and held an almost angelic aura, a warmth so alluring he couldn't stop staring.

"He's some kind of addict," a woman in front of him said to the lady getting her order filled.

Henry shifted from one foot to the other. The pathetic looks he got from the customers seated at the tables almost sent him out the door. The residents of Plain City weren't going to hold any punches. They were going to humble him every chance they could. Maybe though, that'd be a good thing to keep him on track. And frankly, he deserved it.

"You're next, Carol," that sweet voice said, causing the older lady with the big mouth to shuffle forward. Talk about perfect timing.

Henry gave the beauty behind the counter an appreciative smile, which she returned. She had a calming presence. And was pretty and wholesome with light blonde hair, pulled tightly back into a ponytail, emphasizing her heart-shaped face. Her cheekbones were high and structured, her nose pert and slightly upturned. All pulled together by those amazing green eyes. Henry was entranced—drawn to her like a newsman to a once in a lifetime byline.

"You're next," she said, biting her full bottom lip.

Henry swallowed hard and glanced at the menu above her head. "What do you recommend?"

"Our house blend coffee is our best seller. The bear claws are scrumptious."

He returned his attention to her. "Sounds good. Make the coffee large and give me two of the bear claws."

"Coming right up." As she rushed to retrieve his order, his gaze held fast to her. He found himself mesmerized by the way she moved—the way her hands lingered on everything she touched.

5

Back at the counter, she handed him a paper cup and a white bag. "Seeing as you are new and all, this one's on the house."

That was a first. Getting something for nothing. What was the catch? "Are you sure?"

"This way you'll feel obligated to come back."

Good marketing strategy. He'd have to remember that. "Thanks."

Reluctantly, he turned to leave. Hell, he could have stayed and absorbed more of her positive energy. But right now, he had to get to work and hope something exciting happened in this tiny, hole-in-the-wall town. If not, he was going to shrivel up and die before he turned forty.

Outside, as he headed to his car, an ambulance flew by with no lights on.

Henry rubbed his jaw. The way he looked at this, he had two options. Number one, go into the office and sit around. Or two, chase a story. This was a no-brainer.

He jumped in the driver's seat and followed the emergency vehicle out of city limits.

The winding roads were something else he would have to get used to, he thought, maneuvering to a crawl not to run into the ditch. No way would he even try to drink his coffee, let alone eat.

Fifteen minutes into the crazy ride, red taillights came on in front of him.

Henry stomped on the brakes.

The ambulance took a turn onto a dirt drive that hadn't been traveled recently. Waist-high grass slapped beneath the vehicle. Evergreen and oak trees lined both sides of the road. Henry was surprised anyone would even be able to find the place, and now that he looked around, he didn't see any phone or power lines running down this way. How did someone call for assistance? Maybe a cell phone. But would they have any bars this far out? He reached for his phone, finding no service.

The ambulance again slowed its roll and jutted right.

He did the same, his gaze widening when he saw four patrol cruisers parked off to the left of a weathered barn, red, peeling paint in areas, the roof of the structure sagging on one side. He'd have second thoughts about going into the place, afraid it might collapse. But police officers were inside.

Yellow crime scene tape had been strung up. However, he wondered why, since he was sure no one ever came out here. Besides this crew. Everywhere, reeds and grass were trampled down leading to the barn.

He backed his car behind a few trees and reached for his coffee. He'd watch what was going on. Crime tape meant someone was dead. So then, why call an ambulance instead of a coroner? Maybe they were trying to keep this under wraps. Which meant there was a story here, but could he get close enough to find out what it was?

He grabbed the bag off the passenger seat, snatched one of the bear claws, and took a bite, his taste buds going wild. The pretty, green-eyed blonde wasn't lying. The doughy confection felt like an orgasm in his mouth.

As he continued to stuff his face, he kept an eye peeled on the scene in front of him. Both EMTs stepped inside the barn, and only moments later, one rushed out and heaved onto the ground to the right side.

Jesus. Henry needed to get inside and see what made that man sick. It had to be horrendous since they were used to seeing awful sights.

7

He placed his coffee back into the cup holder, scarfed down the rest of the donut, and reached in the back floorboard for his camera. Outside the car, he headed toward the rickety structure. His intent was to stay low so he wouldn't be seen.

The EMT who'd puked had gone inside again, and Henry snuck around the left side, hoping there was another way in.

The grass stood shoulder-height toward the back, thicker and harder to wade through, probably filled with chiggers.

A window with no glass on the far side of the building caught his attention, and he worked his way toward it. As he neared the sill, he heard voices from inside.

"We need to keep this contained. If anything gets out, we'll have a shit storm to deal with," a deep, male voice said.

Henry couldn't believe his luck. The first day on the job and this fell into his lap. Now, if he could find out what it was, he'd have a caption for the newspaper in the morning, one that would probably rival any Plain City had ever had in the past. And with pictures, he'd be in journalistic heaven.

At the window, Henry peeked inside. The sight that met him drained the blood from his extremities, and the coffee and donut in his stomach working its way back up his throat.

****

A knock at the door of the coffeehouse's kitchen had Blake Allen glancing at her teenage employee, who was washing up the last of the dirty dishes in the sink. "Could you get that, Amy? My hands are full," she said, kneading the dough on the large, stainless-steel table centered in the middle of the room.

"Yep." The lanky eighteen-year-old wiped her hands on a towel and headed toward the back.

"Are you finished yet?" Blake heard as Amy returned with her best friend, Sara in tow, a girl who was the polar opposite of her employee.

Sara Shelby barely reached five feet. She was curvy from top to bottom and had a much more guarded personality than her counterpart. That was the reason Blake had chosen Amy over her when both had applied for the part-time position at the coffee shop. She needed bubbly and outgoing for her line of work.

"Hey, how's your mother doing?" Blake asked her while studying the girl's face. Something about her seemed different, but she couldn't put a finger on what.

The dishwater blonde wrinkled her freckled nose. "She's the same. Crazy busy as always. Today, she's working on completing *'her list'* of things to do and bring to the social Sunday. You know she's never happy unless she's working on something. Speaking of work, is Amy done for the day? We have plans, and if we don't hurry, we're going to be late."

Amy looked at Blake for an answer.

"Go ahead. I'm just going to finish up here. I'll see you tomorrow morning, then?"

"Yep. See you. Oh, can I grab a bear claw to take with me?"

"Of course. Get one for Sara as well and enjoy your evening."

Both girls grabbed a pastry and headed for the back door, giggling as they left.

Blake was once like that. Carefree and excited about

going out and experiencing new things. It seemed so long ago now. Once you hit adulthood, time moved quickly. Maybe too quickly.

She blew out a breath and wiped a shirt-sleeved arm across her brow.

The prep work for the morning rush was the last thing she had to do before closing for the day, after a morning and afternoon that had been more hectic than usual. Not a bad thing, just wearing on her twenty-nine-year-old body.

While owning her own business was rewarding, it too was challenging with only herself and Amy, who only worked two hours before school, an hour after, two days a week, then five hours on Saturday. Blake was there Monday through Saturday. Dusk to dawn.

Her only day off was Sunday. Though, for the last two weeks, she'd played the organ for the church services since Beverly Clarence abruptly quit. Rumor was that Bev and the new pastor, Gabriel Huntington, hadn't clicked and the older woman decided to step down from a job she'd held for the past thirty years. Her resignation had come as quite a shock to the Plain City Fellowship Church parishioners, but the change hadn't hurt anything. Their congregation had tripled in size since Pastor Gabriel had taken to the pulpit. He was a charismatic man, younger, and had everyone focused on his sermons. Or maybe it was just the women who held on to his every word. Blake wasn't sure. He certainly was handsome, with his head of curly, almost shoulder-length hair and intense, hazel eyes. But for Blake, his looks didn't matter. It was how he'd brought so many people into the pews every Sunday. After all, that was the goal of a Christian, to convert more souls to God.

His style was so different than the former pastor's. Kirkland Ames had forty-plus years on Gabriel, and a younger man oozed more enthusiasm and energy. Something Blake liked. That's why, when asked to take Beverly's place, she hadn't hesitated to say yes.

Her cell phone went off and brought her back to the dough she'd been working and the sticky mess on her hands. Whoever was trying to call was going to have to wait until she'd finished and washed up.

Twenty minutes later, she covered the huge bowl of dough with plastic wrap, carried it to the refrigerator, and placed it inside. Early in the morning, she'd take it out to allow the dough to rise so she could make fresh donuts for the day.

She reached into her purse for her phone and keys to leave. One missed call from Jenell. She pressed phone option and waited for her to answer. On the fifth ring, Jenell picked up. "Finally."

Blake squinted as she stepped outside and locked the door. "What's going on?"

"I was wondering if you'd heard from Beverly the past couple of days. I've been trying to call her, but I get no answer."

"No, and now that I think about it, she wasn't at church Sunday either, was she?"

"I don't remember, but Charlene Filmore called me, concerned. They were supposed to go to bingo at the Elks, but she never showed up. She dropped by Bev's place, but her car was gone."

"That's odd." Blake leaned against the back door, anxiously kicking at the gravel on the ground. "If she was going out of town, surely she would have told someone."

"That's why Charlene called me. She thought maybe I'd know something since I live a few houses down from her."

Blake pushed away from the door and stepped over to her car. "When was the last time you saw her?"

"Saturday afternoon, I think. She was leaving the subdivision and she didn't look happy."

"Okay, so maybe she was called away on an emergency." Blake inhaled a breath. "Perhaps she hasn't had time to tell anyone."

"You're probably right. Charlene is just being a worrywart. So, are we still on for a movie tonight?"

"Yep. I've just finished up here. I'm going home to change. Then I'll pick you up."

"Oh, hey, have you met the new guy in town yet?" Jenell asked, her voice now filled with excitement. "The so-called fallen journalist? I heard he's quite the looker."

"He came in for coffee this morning."

"And…"

"And, what?"

"Is he cute?"

"I don't know. I guess if you like the straight out of bed look."

"Oooh, sounds intriguing. I can't wait to meet him."

Blake sighed. Same old Jenell. Jumping in headfirst. Blake had learned to avoid that early on. Too bad it had taken a traumatic experience to do so. "Do you remember what we talked about when you and Trent ended things? You can't fix someone who's broken, Nell. According to the AP, this guy is a recovering oxycodone addict."

"Yes, I know, but aren't you always saying that God forgives and so should we? That everyone deserves a second chance?"

"Yes, that's true, but trusting a man like that is another thing altogether, especially when it comes to personal failings that could bleed into your own life. I know that sounds judgmental. I just don't want that for you. You suffered enough with your ex and his gambling problem. You need a man to care for you, to support your goals, not one you must watch 24/7."

"I'd rather have to babysit than not want one at all. Loneliness isn't all it's cracked up to be, is it?"

"Oh, Jenell, I wish you'd see how wrong you are. If you need a man so desperately, why can't you at least be attracted to a nice guy with a good job?"

"What's the fun in that?"

This was what Blake dealt with all the time with her best friend. She didn't care how appealing a man was, and Henry Kiel had that going for him, but addiction was a deal-breaker. Horrible things happened when mind-altering drugs came into play, things that could change lives forever. So, forgiveness was one thing, but trusting in someone with vices wasn't something Blake was willing to do on blind faith. Not after what happened to her.

Chapter Two

Henry pushed the heavy, glass door to the *Tribune* open and stepped inside, wishing he could erase what he had seen earlier. Over his ten years in journalism, he'd witnessed many horrific sights, from suicide bombings to beheadings, yet none had the effect of him like this had. A murder so appalling that it had no place on the cover of a newspaper anywhere in the world.

No wonder the police wanted to keep the grisly killing quiet. The horrible death could panic the whole town—the entire state of Arkansas if the specifics got out. And here, he thought Plain City would be dull as paint drying. Not after this.

"Where the hell have you been? You need to know right here and now we don't make our own hours. This job is nine to five, six days a week." Simon Ridge stalked toward Henry, his gray eyes wide, almost bulging from their sockets, a hard grimace stretched across his lips. "If you can't live with that, we might as well part ways now."

What could Henry say? How well would hire and fired on the same day look on a resume? Especially with his rehab adventure. It's not like he could tell Simon what he'd seen. Not yet. He'd need to talk to the sheriff first. Though, maybe he could give him a hint of a huge story to come. It might work to keep his job.

"Look, here's what happened, Simon. I stepped out

of Allen's after getting coffee and spotted an ambulance whipping by without any lights. I thought there could be a story."

Simon slammed his hands on his hips. "And…?"

Jesus. Henry was screwed. Whatever he said would have consequences. "There's a story, Simon. I just need to work on sources. Give me until Friday to get some preliminaries on this."

His editor squinted this time, clearly debating whether to believe him. "All right. I'll expect something early Friday morning. Get to work on those sources. This better be good."

"I think you'll be happy." Henry walked down the narrow hallway to his partitioned area—a five by five cubicle that would have made him claustrophobic a year ago. But since his stint in rehab, the small area felt somehow comforting.

He wasn't sure if the sheriff would even talk to him about the victim inside the barn, but he had to try, or Plain City would be in his rearview mirror before he'd had a chance to get used to those damned crickets. If he blew this, he doubted Simon would welcome him back. Not with that short fuse. Henry would need to watch his step.

He gathered up a notebook, pens, and a small voice recorder, then started back toward the door.

You'll get one chance. Don't screw it up.

Back inside his car, Henry reached for his phone and found the police station's address on his location app. If he lived here, he'd be working hand in hand with the authorities, and he might as well get started.

The address came up. A block over.

Every nerve in his body charged. What if they

refused to see things Henry's way? Could they have him arrested for trespassing at a crime scene? He didn't know.

Then again, he could say that no police tape circled the back. *Like that'd matter.*

Why hadn't he just ignored the ambulance and gone straight to work? Done his nine to five in complete boredom, writing about the water main break off Cisco that flooded the local feed store. If he had, he wouldn't be in this dilemma now. Simon wouldn't be about to pop a blood vessel and expect a story by Friday. An article he might not be able to get any information on. It was entirely up to the sheriff. Too bad Henry's nosey nature had always been in his blood—a trait that made him a great journalist but lousy in any other aspect of his life.

The goal in his field had always been to get to the truth, which would be no different here. Henry needed to find out what happened in that dilapidated barn, no matter how difficult or career-ending that might be. Worst come to worst, he'd start over a third time.

Exhaling a deep sigh, Henry started his car. A swirl of ideas on how to broach the topic of murder to the sheriff ran a marathon in his mind. He didn't even know who ran the police department in town. Under normal circumstances, he'd have casually met the man before dealing with a story surrounding him.

This was anything but normal.

He pulled into a spot in the visitor parking area across the street from the station, got out, pressing the lock door button on his key fob. This had to be handled delicately or shit might fly, or fists, and the cops would target him for the duration of his stay in Plain City. Neither he nor the sheriff needed that. They probably already thought of him as a lowlife because of his past. Henry didn't want to make matters worse.

The police station itself stood three stories high, gray brick, with a dome type top. Historically old yet nicely kept. Ten steps led to the front doors, and Henry took them one at a time.

Once inside, he walked straight ahead to the glass divider where a uniformed officer sat.

"Can I help you?" The man gave Henry an up and down appraisal.

"I'd like to speak to the sheriff."

"He's not available right now. Can I ask what this is about?"

"I need to speak to him privately. It's about an old barn."

The officer's cheeks lost a little color, and his eyes narrowed. "Who are you?"

"Name's Henry Kiel. I'm the new reporter at the *Tribune*."

The man paled even more.

"Take a seat in my eyesight, Mr. Kiel," he said as he picked up the phone on his desk. "I'll see if the sheriff's out of his meeting."

Henry stepped over to the waiting area and sat, his heart racing in his chest. His plan wasn't going to go well if the officer's reaction meant anything. He glanced back at the man and received a heated glare in response.

Yep. Deep shit.

Henry pulled his phone from the back pocket of his jeans and swiped his e-mail app.

Once it came up, a subject line immediately caught his attention, and he opened the message from his sister.

A sinking feeling made his gut clench. He hadn't

spoken to Karen in over a year, not since his decline. And she wasn't the only one. His family thought him a lost cause after the accident, and he could live with that since he deserved their ire. Who'd want to be around someone with such deep flaws? A weakness that none of his family had ever experienced.

I thought I should let you know mom isn't well. Daddy said there was no need for you to come home but thought you should know about it.

Karen

His stomach wrenched tighter. When was the last time he'd seen his mother? He really didn't remember. Maybe a few months before the accident. She'd looked frail then. Guilt closed off his throat, and he swallowed hard, forcing himself to take a breath. Okay, perhaps going home right now wasn't feasible, but a phone call to his parents wouldn't hurt. "Mr. Kiel," a man asked, drawing him out of his troubled thoughts.

The voice from inside the barn.

Henry glanced up to find an older man, a few inches over six feet and quite fit for his age, staring down at him. A pair of metal-rimmed spectacles sat on his hawk-like nose, highlighting the man's questioning, hazel eyes.

"I'm Sheriff Grandy. You needed to talk to me?"

"Yes." Henry stood. "Could we go somewhere private?"

He nodded. "Let's head to my office."

Henry followed him down a long hallway and up two flights of stairs to a large, dark-paneled room with a row of windows off to one side. "Take a seat. Could I offer you a cup of coffee?"

"Sure," he said, feeling a bit winded from the climb.

Grandy walked to a buffet type table with a

microwave and a coffeemaker and poured two cups.

"Cream or sugar?"

"Black's fine."

The sheriff came over and handed him one, then went to sit behind his desk.

Henry took a sip and waited for the man to do the same. "So, what brings you here today?"

"First, I want you to know I'm here to help you, sheriff."

"What can you help me with, Mr. Kiel?"

Henry shifted in his chair. "Let me start from the beginning."

The man thrummed his fingers on the desk. "All right."

"I was leaving Allen's this morning when I saw an ambulance fly by me. Being a journalist, I thought there could be a story. I followed it."

"And," the sheriff said, his gaze intent on him.

"I know what you found in that barn, sheriff. Let me help you find the murderer."

"Look, Mr. Kiel, you might have gotten stories this way in the cities you've worked before, but it's not going to work with me. Frankly, I could have you arrested for chasing down an emergency vehicle."

Henry shifted and cleared his throat. "I know this is something you don't want to get out. I don't blame you, sheriff. That's the last thing I want. I simply want to help. Let me do some digging into the victim. Maybe I can find something you can use."

The sheriff straightened in his chair. "So, let's say, I allow you to do this. What do you get in return?"

"I want to be able to tell the story when it's all said and done. That's it. I won't write anything until the case is solved. You have my word on that."

"Yes, but can I trust your word, Mr. Kiel? That's the question."

Henry cleared his throat again. "I assume you're saying you don't trust me because of my past? Right?"

"I've heard the rumors and couldn't care less about your drug abuse problems. That's your own issue as far as I'm concerned. It's the fact that you're a journalist. The last guy who held your job screwed a deal that the city had with a business opportunity. It cost us hundreds of new jobs and thousands of dollars in revenue. I don't trust a man whose livelihood is based on a byline."

"Okay, I get that you don't trust me, but you have my word that I won't publish anything at the *Tribune* that isn't run by you first. Allow me to use my abilities as an investigative journalist to find this killer."

Grandy leaned back in his chair and rubbed at the gray stubble on his chin.

As seconds ticked by, sweat beaded on Henry's upper lip.

"All right, Mr. Kiel," the sheriff said in a resigned tone. "I'll agree to let you do some digging into our victim's life. No one can know about it, though. Will that be a problem?"

"Not at all. If you could write down whatever information you'll allow me to have, I'll get out of your hair."

"The sheriff scribbled on a Post-It note then slid it to him. "I hope I won't regret this."

"You won't." Henry rose and reached out to shake the sheriff's hand, then turned to leave. Sheriff Grandy had given him this opportunity. For the sake of his sanity, he needed this investigation to keep him busy and get him through his days in journalist purgatory. He wasn't going to let anything blow this for him. Not when it was the only way to get his old life back.

****

Blake pulled a tray of apple turnovers out of the oven and placed it on the layered rack against the wall. They were the last to come out before she could open for the morning. Three of her coffee makers were brewing, along with the one she used to heat water for tea.

She rolled the rack toward the front to load her display case. Once filled, she wheeled the cart back into the kitchen and glanced at the clock on the wall. She had fifteen minutes until she opened.

She rushed to the restroom to tidy up. This morning was going to be incredibly stressful since Amy hadn't shown up for work. She'd tried calling her to find out if she'd slept in, but she never answered her phone. Her employee had never been late, let alone not come in, or not called to say she wasn't coming in. Her absence made Blake worried.

As she was washing her hands, a knock sounded on the outer door. *Amy!* Maybe she had car trouble and forgot to charge her phone.

In the front, she glanced out the window, and her relief turned to confusion. It wasn't Amy but the girl's mother.

Blake unlocked the bolt lock and opened the door.

"Is Amy here?" the older woman asked, rushing inside.

"No. She hasn't shown up to work yet. I called but got no answer."

Deana Maness wrung her hands, her eyes flooding with tears. "She's been acting strange the last couple of days and then didn't come home last night. I thought for sure she'd be here. I'm scared something's happened to her."

"Have you called Sara? The two left together yesterday afternoon. Said they had plans. Maybe she stayed with her last night?"

"That's the first thing I did. Sara didn't answer her phone, either. I left a voicemail. That was hours ago."

"Maybe the two are out of range somewhere together. Some places out of town, you lose cell service."

"I hope you're right. It's not like Amy Jo to do something like this."

"I agree." Blake nodded. "She's never missed a day of work without calling in. It must be something out of her control."

"What if they were in an accident and are lying in a ravine somewhere. Could the police locate the girls by their cell phones?"

Blake nodded. "I think so, as long as they're on."

"I'll stop in and talk to the sheriff."

"Let me know what he says. And I'll call you immediately if she shows up here."

"All right." Amy's mother left her coffee shop, turning left toward the police station.

Blake paced the floor in front of the counter. The whole thing seemed uncharacteristic of Amy, and her mother had every reason to be concerned. She said a quick prayer that everything would turn out all right, then went to switch on the open sign. Today was going to be crazy, being on her own all day for two-for-Tuesday. She was glad she'd made extra of everything just in case it got hectic.

No sooner had she unlocked the door when Mr. Kiel

walked in, his hair spiking every direction. Had he done it on purpose?

"Good morning." He stepped closer to the front counter.

"What can I get for you today?"

"I'll have some of your house coffee for now. I was hoping to pick your brain on some of the people in town since you own the most popular place in Plain City."

"I don't know about that." Blake had never been a gossip, despised it in fact, and that was never going to change.

"Now, you're just being modest." He flashed her a bright smile that sent an internal warning sign flashing in the back of Blake's brain. Good-looking men used a half-hearted grin, a wink or two, and some mild flirtation to gain the upper hand. Nothing like that worked on Blake. Not since her teen years. Once burned, she'd learned her lesson. She wanted honesty and a good heart, and that proved hard to come by these days. Everyone seemed out for themselves.

She stepped over to the coffee machines and poured him a cup of French blend and placed a lid on top. "That will be two-fifty."

He gave her three crisp dollar bills. "Keep the change."

She handed him the coffee and a strange sensation shot through her body from the simple brush of his hand. Shocked, she glanced at him, noting no reaction.

"Do you know who owns the land out off highway Z? The one that has the old, red barn ready to collapse?"

Blake frowned. "Why do you ask?"

"Just curious. I took a drive out that way and ended up there."

She studied his face. He really looked handsome with his big, chocolate-brown eyes that held an intensity she found almost unnerving—probably the reason he had been so good at his job before his problems brought him down.

"Harold Linder owned it before he died two years ago. He had no family I knew of. So, I have no idea who owns it now. I'm sure you could go to the courthouse and find out."

He smiled again. "I did. Supposedly, it's in the hands of some corporate trust."

"If you knew that, then why ask me?"

"Because Bolton, Inc. doesn't really tell you anything. I thought maybe you'd heard rumors about who is behind the name."

Wow. Why would Henry Kiel think she'd tell him anything if she even knew? Blake had no idea of this man's real character besides being a journalist who used to work for a large news organization.

"Sorry. I can't help you." Blake was thankful when someone else came through the door. This conversation unsettled her.

"Have a nice day," she said to him, rushing to get Steven Pruell's usual. Coffee with her signature cinnamon rolls times two.

When she returned to the counter, Kiel had ducked out the door. For whatever reason, the man suggesting she'd know all the gossip in town upset her. Busy-bodies irritated Blake, especially with all the rumors of her and Billy Caine in high school—all horrible lies. So, for Kiel to assume she was like that only disturbed her more, and Blake hoped he never returned. She didn't need his business—tingle or no tingle.

Chapter Three

Henry seemed to be striking out left and right. The owner of the coffeehouse had looked downright offended when he'd asked her about the old barn. Could she possibly not know anything? Or was she like everyone else in Plain City with their apparent dislike of his profession and not want to tell him anything? Even the clerk at the assessor's office eyed him with judgment—like he was the reporter who'd cost them the new jobs in town. It wasn't going to be easy to earn people's trust here, which would slow progress in finding the killer.

In his car, he leaned back against the leather seat and closed his eyes. Pain pounded away at his temples and made his irises sensitive to the bright sunlight. He hoped caffeine would somehow ease the throbbing.

As he went for a sip of coffee, a loud tapping on his driver's window made him jolt and slosh the hot liquid onto his crotch, the burning sensation making him squirm and pull the scalding denim away from his skin. "Son of a…"

The tapping started again.

He turned toward his window and found a redhead standing next to his car, leaning over, her shirt gaped open. She signaled for him to roll down his window. He pushed the button, and the tinted glass slid down as he took a slow, even breath, hoping the coffee wouldn't blister his skin.

"Are you Henry Kiel?" The question came out in a rush.

"Yeah. Why?"

She stuck her hand in the window, waiting for him to shake it. "Hi. My name's Jenell Kilmer. I've been looking forward to meeting you. It's not every day you get to greet a celebrity in Plain City."

He clasped his palm into hers, then let go. "I wouldn't say I'm a celebrity. Infamous, maybe."

She laughed, revealing straight, super-white teeth.

Nice to know someone there got his sense of humor. So far, everyone in the southern Arkansas town seemed void of even an ounce of wit. Then again, what could be funny while stuck in this speck on a map? Bingo at the Elks supposedly the highlight of the week. How could he contain himself?

"Anyway, I know you have things to do, but I thought maybe I could invite you to a social this weekend. It'd give you a chance to meet some of the residents of the community."

Was she asking him out? Not that it mattered. Her invitation was his way to get some information. "What kind of social?"

"Church. Right after Sunday services."

Henry's heart sank. When was the last time he'd been inside a church? *The one burned out by Turkish rebels didn't count, did it? Probably not.*

Hell, he'd prefer Bingo.

"You don't have to attend services if that's your hesitation. You can just come after. A lot of people do."

Wow, the woman could read minds. He'd better watch his back with this one. The last thing he needed was someone knowing his every thought. Like his mother had when he was growing up. All he'd had to do was think about doing something wrong, and she'd been there to stop him. If only she'd come to Nigeria with him, she might have been able to talk some sense into him. Make him realize it was a trap. Maverick would be here now if she had.

"All right. I'll come. Where is the event being held?"

She took a pad and pen out of her handbag, jotted something down, then tore it off and handed it to him. "It starts at noon. I look forward to seeing you there."

"Okay. Sunday then."

Henry closed the window and took a sip of his coffee, watching as the woman stepped into Allen's. She had a nice body, but he wasn't interested in her in that way. The blonde working behind the counter of the shop Miss Kilmer just walked into stirred emotion inside him. It was all in those eyes of hers—a warmth beyond anything he'd ever encountered—beckoning to him in some way.

Henry quickly shook the thought. He had more important things to do now. He needed to find someone who knew the dead woman, and who might have had a need to see her torn in two.

He started the car, debating on where to go from here. First, he'd check in at the paper. Maybe his editor had some idea as to who the man behind the corporation could be. That seemed to be a place to start since the victim was found on that property. Maybe later in the day, he'd check out her home, though he was sure Grandy had done that already.

Wait a minute. Who found the body in the first

place? A question for the sheriff. Maybe that should be his next step—back to talk to Grandy. Perhaps the person who found the murdered victim knew something they weren't willing to tell the authorities. Henry had a way to get people to talk. That's how he had earned all his journalist awards over the years. Hopefully, it'd work to get him what he needed now.

His goal set, Henry pulled away from the curb and took the first right on his way to the police station. As he drove into the parking area, he spotted the sheriff crossing the street toward his patrol car. Henry parked and raced across the road to get to him. "Sheriff," he called right as Grandy opened his car door.

The man turned, his eyes narrowed. Henry was clearly the last person the sheriff wanted to see.

"What can I do for you, Kiel?" His pleasant tone seemed forced.

"Can you tell me who found the victim?"

"I don't know. We got a call from an untraceable number to go check out the barn."

"Don't you find that strange?"

The sheriff blew out a heavy breath. "Strange? Hum. What's strange, Kiel is the killing itself. I'm having a hard time wrapping my head around someone doing something so horrific to another person. So, yeah, the whole thing is strange. Bizarre. Off-the-wall, freakishly unusual, or any other adjectives you want to attach to it."

Henry had to agree. "Right. Dumb question."

"Is that all you wanted because I have a killer to catch. Oh and, not pointing out the obvious, but you might want to change your pants. It looks like you pissed them."

Henry glanced down at his crotch. "Yeah, I spilled

my coffee."

The sheriff opened his door wider. "Hmmm, whatever, Kiel. We both have jobs to do now, don't we? Might want to get on that."

"Wait, one more question. Did you find anything at the woman's home?"

The sheriff shook his head. "Not anything that could lead to who killed her, no."

"Okay. Thanks."

Grandy slammed his car door and started the engine.

Henry moved aside to allow him to pull away, then stared up at the blue sky for a moment or two. The sheriff didn't like him. Hell, most of the time, Henry didn't like himself, his absence of common sense and control at the center of it all. One only had to look at his relationship with his own family to see he lacked the emotional connection gene since visiting hadn't been a priority. His camera man, and best friend Maverick, had somehow broken through that cold exterior, and Henry missed having him around. To talk everything through with him. The man had had a way of knowing what direction to go. A sixth sense of sorts. Hell, he'd tried to talk Henry out of going to Nigeria. If only he'd listened.

Emotion clogged his throat as he returned to his car. He'd go back to his original plan once he went home to change. Hopefully, his editor could give him a direction to go forward. Otherwise, he was back to square one with no clue as to which way to go next.

****

"You did what?" Blake asked in a much sharper voice than she'd intended.

"I said," Jenell repeated, seemingly unfazed by her curtness. "I invited the new guy to the Sunday social, and he accepted."

Blake turned away. She didn't want to go into this discussion further. Something about Henry Kiel grated on her nerves, but she refused to say that. Knowing Jenell as well as Blake did, she would probably blurt it out to the man, and whoever else was in listening distance. That was the last thing Blake needed.

"What do you have against this guy, anyway?" Jenell stepped behind the counter to face her.

"Nothing. I don't want you jumping in headfirst again like you always do. The guy has some major problems. That's the last thing you want."

"For someone so in touch with your spiritual side, Blake, I'd think you'd be a little more understanding." Her best friend's amber eyes met hers with an intensity she'd never seen from her before.

Maybe she was right that Blake was overly critical of Mr. Kiel. She'd need to do some much-needed soul searching on why.

"Okay, but don't come crying to me when he turns out to be Mister Wrong again."

"I promise I won't. Now, I have the day off and it looks like it's going to get busy." Jenell pointed toward the picture window, where Blake saw a line of people forming outside the door. "I'll stay and help."

"You're a Godsend."

"Yes, I am, and don't you forget that."

For three hours, they raced the floors to wait on people, and when Blake finally had a slow period, the two plopped down to sip at their coffee.

"How do you do this every day?" Jenell slumped against the seatback.

"It's not like this all the time. Just two-for-Tuesdays

and some Saturdays."

"I feel like I ran a fifteen-mile marathon."

"Ha! How could you possibly know that? In high school, you'd get a stitch in your side from the fifty-yard dash."

Jenell stuck out her tongue. "Next time you need help, I'll leave you to do it yourself, you ungrateful scallywag."

Blake burst out laughing. Some of the things her friend said were from the books she'd been reading that month. Jenell must be in her historical romance phase again. Much, much better than when she'd been perusing Fifty Shades of mortifying. Her colorful language would get her banned from the local shops and left Blake all shades of red.

"How'd you manage to get the day off?" Blake took another swallow of coffee.

"Dean called me early this morning and said that he wasn't opening up and I could enjoy a paid day without putting in the work."

"Don't you find that a little odd considering the man never closes, even in bad weather?"

"If he's working at Miller Accounting, I am too, so yes, it's odd, but I wasn't about to insist he come in. I'd much rather be running around here than there, trying to stay awake. The man is ridiculously boring. I mean, counting numbers all day is tedious enough. Throw old stick in the mud into the mix, and it's a recipe for the worst case of narcolepsy. I can see why he's been single all these years. Who'd want to live with that day in and day out? It'd be, Snoresville, USA."

Blake snorted. This was why she loved Jenell. Even as embarrassing as she could be on a good day, she always managed to put a smile on Blake's face. Yet, why had Dean Miller closed his business for the day? It was so uncharacteristic of the older man and strangely odd, though that seemed to have become the norm since the new guy showed up to Plain City. Blake couldn't decide if that was good or bad—she'd have to wait and see what happened Sunday after Church.

Chapter Four

Henry looked at all the cars in the parking area and almost turned around. The church was clearly a popular hangout. He wasn't sure he could deal with so many people all at once. Since the explosion that killed his friend, large crowds caused him extreme anxiety.

That day would live in infamy for him. He and Maverick had been following two busloads of refugees to research a story, at a camp of *Doctors without Borders*—almost everyone killed in the bombing. So, any clustering of people triggered the memory—issues he'd over-medicated himself from until rehab. Now, he needed to cope in other ways. Slow belly meditation, and serene imagery helped when he felt a full-blown panic attack coming on. Picturing wave after wave of deep blue ocean slapping a sandy beach, seafoam bubbling on the edge of the shoreline, the water rolling over and over in his mind—all the while breathing even and slow.

Henry drove into the area and found a place in the back to park.

Early that morning, he'd considered staying home. He'd thought about calling his sister instead to find out how their mother was doing since that email days ago. But this might be his only opportunity to learn if anyone knew who owned the land where the barn sat. His editor had no clue and was none too pleased that come Friday, he couldn't tell him anything about the story he'd been working on. He told Simon he wasn't allowed to say a word yet.

The only reason he still had a job today was because he offered to do a piece on the social event. That seemed to appease Simon for the time being. But, if Henry didn't uncover something soon, Sheriff Grandy might run him out of town anyway.

He followed the path to the back of the large white church. Not one of those new age looking structures, but an older building that had a steepled roof with a bell on top.

He rounded the corner and was taken aback by the number of people, some eating at long tables, others standing in groups behind them, chatting. Another set, off to the left, tossing bean bags toward a set of square boxes with holes in the middle. Everyone wore bright, happy smiles. What the hell could they be so happy about?

As Henry took in the sights and sounds around him, his chest started to tighten. *Breathe. Slow. Even. Again. One more time. Now, think of something pleasant.* The blonde from the coffee shop came to mind, a thought that had him shaking his head. Sure, she was pretty, but right now, he needed to find the woman who'd invited him to the social so she could introduce him to some of the people here. The job was his number one priority, and nothing else mattered, especially since *that job* was on the line.

He scanned the groups standing first, then the three long tables, his attention landing on the blonde coffee shop owner. *It figures she'd be here.* Next to her was the redhead. Were the two friends? Did it matter?

Henry swallowed hard and made his way toward

Jenell, his step faltering when a tall man in black, with a head of curly dark hair, came to stand next to the blonde, leaning over to whisper something in her ear. Her lips parted, and she smiled, her reaction leaving a bad taste in Henry's mouth.

Who was this person? Her boyfriend? Husband? Henry hadn't noticed a ring on her finger.

The guy turned, and he saw the white collar. *The pastor.* But was he more than that to her? He seemed hands-on, touching her shoulder, but maybe he was that way toward everyone. Henry would keep an eye on him and watch them before he came to any conclusions. Not that it mattered either way.

"Funny seeing you here, Kiel." Henry turned to find the sheriff a few feet away, out of uniform, holding a plate of food.

He stepped over to him. "Sheriff Grandy. Jenell Kilmer asked me to come. This your church?"

"Nope. I was invited, as well. You able to learn anything, yet?"

Henry shook his head. "I thought maybe by coming here today, I could get some leads."

Grandy rubbed at his chin, then glanced around, his gaze intense.

"Are you looking for someone?"

The sheriff's features showed no reaction. "I was hoping to see a couple of the local girls. They've been laying low for a few days."

"You don't think that something—"

Grandy raised his hand to stop him. "We don't want anyone overhearing anything."

Henry wondered if the sheriff knew something he didn't. Was he there watching someone? Or was he indeed looking for these missing girls?

"Can we talk later?"

"We'll speak when I have something to say, Kiel. Right now, I just plan to eat. Go meet up with Jenell. I'm sure she's excited about showing you off."

Okay. That was a definite, *get lost* if he'd ever heard one. Not to mention making him sound like some prized pig.

Henry angled between two of the tables and tapped on the redhead's shoulder. The excitement in her eyes when she saw him was unmistakable. He didn't want to use her, but her interest in him could come in handy. She knew people in town. Henry could utilize that since no one wanted to talk to him openly.

"I wasn't expecting this kind of crowd," he said to her, then glanced at the blonde, who still seemed enthralled with the pastor. In quick succession, he sized the man up. Yep. Better looking than him. Taller. More muscular. Probably never had a drug problem. She'd be dumb not to gravitate toward the guy.

Jenell pulled out the seat next to hers. "I could run and get you a plate of food if you tell me what you'd like."

"No, no, I can do that. Just point me in the right direction."

"I was about to go for dessert. I'll show you."

Henry cleared his throat, hoping to draw the blonde's attention. No such luck. She kept her eyes glued on the man in black. "If you're sure."

Jenell picked her plate up off the table. "I saw a slice of pineapple upside-down cake that has my name on it. Come with me, and I'll introduce you to a few people on the way back."

Henry dutifully followed, catching all the strained looks he received as they passed. At the food line, she handed him plastic silverware wrapped in a napkin and a plate.

He was stunned at all the options, everything from baked ham to green-bean casserole. After filling his plate and grabbing a bottle of water from an iced chest, Jenell led him back toward the table, running into a young couple on the way. "Henry, this is Brent and Carly Stevens. They run the hardware store in town. Carly and Brent, this is our new reporter, Henry Kiel."

"Nice to meet you. I hope you're better than the last guy who had your job," Brent said, his lips turning up into a smirk.

"I'll try my best." *Asshole.* Geez, what was wrong with everyone in this town that they couldn't give a guy a break? Even if he did have a substance abuse problem in his past.

The two laughed and continued to the food table.

"That's the tenth time I've heard about the guy before me. What happened there?" Henry gripped his plate tighter.

"He stuck his nose into something that cost us a new factory just outside of town. It would have grown our city and helped everyone. The company decided to go somewhere else because of his hounding."

"Who was this company, and what was he investigating?"

"Bolton, something or other. They bought a parcel of land a few miles out of Plain City."

What was this journalist's objections to the new company coming to town?

"What happened to the guy? Did he leave town, or

was he forced out?" Henry had to ask since this could very likely be his fate if he didn't find out something to help the sheriff.

"No one knows. He up and disappeared one night."

Henry frowned. "The guy didn't tell anyone he was leaving?"

She shrugged. "Everyone was angry with him. I guess he didn't want to deal with that. Come on, let's go sit down and eat. Your food's getting cold."

The two neared the tables, running into a tall, reed-thin man who gave Jenell a slight smile. "Dean, this is our new newspaper reporter, Henry Kiel."

He nodded his balding head.

"This is my boss, Dean Miller. We're bean counters and do taxes for everyone in town. We'll probably be doing yours if you stay long enough."

"Hello. Did I hear somewhere that you worked overseas news?"

"I was a foreign correspondent, yes."

"Why settle here of all places?" the man asked, his gaze not connecting with Henry's. Why was that? Was he simply asking questions to be polite? Apparently so since his attention was elsewhere.

"Simon offered me a job at the *Tribune*, and I needed to work."

The older man sighed as if he could care less what Henry said. Was he always so rude, or was Dean Miller distracted by something?

"Come on, Henry." Jenell grasped his arm and pulled him away.

"Nice meeting you." Henry waved to the man as they went to sit at the table. They had to move over a seat because the pastor had taken the one next to Blake, the two huddled together talking, in their little world.

Henry concentrated on his plate until the blonde chose that moment to turn to say something to Jenell and spotted him, her mouth dropping open, her eyes narrowing. "Hello." She sounded as thrilled as she looked to see him. The pastor turned as well; the friendly smile he gave Henry not quite ringing true. He reached out his hand to him. "Gabriel Huntington, but everyone calls me Pastor Gabriel."

Henry took ahold of his palm and squeezed a little too tightly, noting how cold the man's touch seemed. Like a reptile. Did that mean anything? Then again, something in his eyes didn't feel right either, strange since he was a man of the cloth. Maybe Henry was simply looking for a gray area that wasn't there. He'd always been good at doing that, according to Maverick.

"You're welcome to join us any Sunday. Services start at ten."

Henry shrugged. "Not much of a churchgoer, but thanks for asking."

"Maybe you could come with Jenell. You might be pleasantly surprised."

Jenell smiled at him, then to the pastor. "I think that's up to him."

Good answer. Henry seriously could warm to her. She might not have those incredible eyes like the blonde coffee shop owner, but she knew how to be diplomatic, and that was a real plus. "We'll see," he said, then went back to eating. "Whoever brought the potato salad needs a pat on the back because I've never had any that tasted this good."

"I made it." Jenell's cheeks turned a pretty shade of pink.

Damn. Another plus. If the woman kept this up, Henry would consider that dating thing. "It's delicious."

"Thanks. It's my mother's recipe. She won a prize for it a few years back."

"I can see why. It's great. So, how long have you lived in Plain City?"

She smiled. "All my life. Blake and I grew up together." She pointed to the blonde. "Been best friends since third grade."

So, that was her name. "Then, you'd know the history of the town?"

"I'm not sure how well, but my mother is on the city council and worked for the county up until she retired last year. What do you need to know?"

Henry had to tread lightly with his questions. "Is she here?"

"Normally, she would be, but she had to go out of town to take care of my uncle who's under the weather. She'll be back day after tomorrow."

He nodded. "I look forward to meeting her." Henry knew he was playing on Jenell's interest. He usually wouldn't do something so underhanded, but he had to find somebody knowledgeable enough about the land that barn sat on, and her mother might just be that person.

****

Blake gathered her things and headed for the parking lot, Pastor Gabriel in tow.

"Thanks again for staying," Gabriel said once they'd reached her SUV.

She shrugged. "I didn't have anything else to do."

"That's hard to believe." His greenish-blue eyes twinkled with amusement. "I know playing the organ for church services takes up your only free time, Blake.

You're a true angel of God to do it."

Blake blushed. A compliment from him meant so much since the man spent every waking moment helping others. She'd seen it with her own eyes. Lights were always on in the church, which meant he was there ministering to someone in need. Pastor Ames had barely made it through church services on Wednesday nights the weeks leading up to his retirement. Their new pastor always seemed available, which helped when you were growing a church.

"I'm here to serve," she said, uncomfortable with the praise.

He smiled. "Not everyone gives up so much to help others. You're a special person."

Yet another compliment. This guy was going to make her head float away.

"I appreciate you saying that. I better get going. I have a few things to do at home. I'll see you Wednesday afternoon."

He reached out and clasped her forearm, the contact causing her to jump back. "I meant to ask you something." His eyes darkened as he released her.

Blake swallowed hard. "What's that?"

"I was hoping that you and I could get dinner one of these evenings. Whenever works for you. I'd like to talk about expanding the music choices for services."

She was somewhat surprised by his idea, but Blake knew she could learn any sheet music given time. The only thing that worried her was being seen in public with him. She'd always had a problem with that. But, maybe with them working together, no one would assume it was anything else but business. Unfortunately, small town people talked. She'd found that out the hard way years ago. "Can I get back to you?"

"Of course. No pressure." He sounded nonchalant, but for some reason, his demeanor seemed less friendly than before. Maybe it was just her imagination. She sometimes let hers run wild. This was probably one of those times.

The silence that remained between them made her uncomfortable. "I'd better go. You have a good evening," she said as she opened her vehicle and got in, clicking her seatbelt in place. Blake prayed that Gabriel hadn't taken her uncertainty as an insult to him in any way. It wasn't. He'd done so much to grow their congregation, and there were rumors of televised services—a boon to any church, anywhere. No one would think anything but wonderful thoughts about him. She just had a problem being seen with any man in public since high school. Not when that meant rumors and innuendoes—the one thing she'd avoided, like the plague since she was seventeen years old and was called a slut by the boy she refused to date. She never wanted a repeat of that.

She swallowed a lump of emotion and backed out of her designated slot in front of the church. Before going home, she planned to stop by Beverly's house to see if she'd gotten home. Blake was concerned for the older woman. It wasn't like her to go off somewhere and not let anyone know. The older woman could have taken a few minutes out of her day to call someone in town to let them know where she'd gone. Then again, Amy and Sara were nowhere to be found either. Where the heck were they?

Could Henry Kiel have something to do with this? Strangely, three reliable people had gone missing within days of his arrival. Could there be a connection?

Blake shook the thought. It was crazy. She was allowing her annoyance with him to cloud her judgment. Maybe she was thinking only about the fact that he was an addict and a journalist. Not about the man himself. Could she know what he was capable of by those standards? No.

Yet, three women had vanished. Where had they gone?

She turned onto Lane Avenue and drove toward Beverly's home, noting a blue Camry parked at Jenell's house. Whose was it? Kiel's?

Blake sighed. Will her best friend ever learn? Why did she always seem to need a man to make her happy? Blake wished she'd find a way to experience joy without a male in the mix.

She parked in Beverly's driveway, walked up to the door, and rang the bell. As she waited, she found herself glancing down the block, wondering what was happening inside Jenell's house. What could her best friend possibly see in Kiel? His hair was always standing on-end, that Kewpie-doll style she never could wrap her head around. He was all kinds of thin—no doubt because of his past addictions. He did have nice eyes, his lashes long and dark. His teeth were straight and white. Okay, maybe he was handsome in an unconventional way, but he lacked control, which was a deal-breaker.

She frowned and rang Bev's doorbell again.

When a door slammed, she turned to see Kiel leaving Jenell's. He stopped when he saw her.

"Hello." He glanced from her to his car, then back again. "Enjoyed the social, though a lot of people make me a little jumpy."

What could she say to that? She had her own issues. "What brings you to Jenell's?" she asked before she could stop herself.

"I helped carry in all the leftovers." He raised a container. "She gave me some of her potato salad."

Blake nodded. "It's a prize winner."

"She told me, and I can believe it. You two are best friends?"

"Yes. For years. Surprisingly, we are opposites. We both wonder how we stay friends when we are so different."

"I had a friend like that. He was so much better than me."

"Was?"

"I gotta go. Have a pleasant evening." He rushed to get to his car.

Blake wasn't sure what she'd said that made him suddenly uncomfortable, but that wasn't her concern.

Blake waved as he drove by, then debated if she should stop in and talk to Jenell. Maybe tell her about Gabriel and what he'd suggested. *Nah.* Her best friend would lecture her on why she didn't say yes. Would scold her for being paranoid again and letting the past get in the way of having a future. It was true. But Blake couldn't help herself. At this point, it was ingrained in her.

She sighed, and she started toward her car, a glint of something in Beverly's grass catching her eye. She padded over to see what it was. An old cell phone lay next to the driveway. It had to be Bev's, but why was it lying in her yard? Could it have fallen out of her purse?

Blake leaned over to pick it up, then tried to turn it on but found the battery dead. Quickly, she stuffed the phone in her purse and walked to her car. This could be why Bev wasn't answering any calls. She didn't have her phone.

Something seemed off, though. Maybe Blake should talk to Sheriff Grandy? Give him the device? Then again, he didn't seem concerned about people going missing. Not when he was enjoying himself at the church's luncheon while three women were nowhere to be found.

Chapter Five

Henry reached across the desk for his cell phone and answered, "Hello."

"Henry, it's Jenell. How are you?"

"I'm doing fine. How about yourself?"

"I'm great. I just wanted to call and let you know that my mom got back last night if you'd like to talk with her. You're welcome to come by for supper. You two could chat after."

He'd been waiting for this call for almost two days now. "Sounds great. Can I bring anything?"

"Just yourself."

He smiled. "I can do that. What time?"

"Seven, okay?"

"Sounds perfect. I'll see you tonight."

"I'm looking forward to it."

Henry ended the call. Surprisingly, he was excited about meeting Jenell's mother. She might be the one person who could tell him something about Bolton Inc., who was behind the name, and what it could have to do with the dead woman. That, and he had begun to like Jenell. The woman was smart and funny—two important qualities.

Unfortunately, she didn't have Blake's eyes or evoke those strange emotions inside him, though he could tell the blonde didn't feel the same. She seemed almost annoyed by him every time they met. He'd enjoyed the conversation they'd shared outside Jenell's house until things got personal. He wasn't ready to talk to anyone in Plain City about Maverick, how his loss had exacerbated his need to medicate further. Just thinking about it sent him racing to his car—with his tail between his legs. She was almost intimidating, something that was foreign to him.

He sighed and rubbed at the tension in his neck. Blake Allen was out of reach for him since she had eyes for Pastor Gabriel and the man certainly had the hots for her. A person would have to be blind not to see it.

He slumped back in his chair. He needed to get to the piece he was writing about the Halloween event details coming next weekend. The article needed to be done and proofed before going to print in the morning. Too bad, his heart wasn't in it. Local happenings were never his thing. He had bigger fish to fry than fish fries, like finding a killer. Hopefully, Jenell's mom could help him there. Someone had to know who bought the property where the barn sat and what they'd planned to do with that land.

Why had they changed their minds about the project?

What was the last journalist's objections to it? Maybe Henry could get the guy's name and forwarding address to ask. Perhaps he could give him some insight into what was wrong with the deal and Plain City itself. Henry had never lived in a small town before. Everything he did and said seemed to be scrutinized, especially by the owner of the only decent coffee shop in town.

"Are you done with that piece yet?" Avery Jones, the copyeditor, asked, startling Henry out of his thoughts.

47

"Give me fifteen more minutes."

The older man adjusted the glasses on his nose then stalked off. Another person who seemed to dislike him. Nothing new.

Henry was doing the best he could. Writing a byline on ISIS affiliates and their movements or even a murder case was one thing. Writing a fluff piece on a city event was a whole different animal. *Don't be arrogant. You're lucky they gave you a job. You could be floundering somewhere, with nothing to do.*

Maybe he could incorporate murder into the fluff. After all, it was Halloween. Why not ramp up the fear factor a bit in the article.

If the town only knew the horror of what had happened two miles out of city limits. They'd be too nervous about letting their kids go trick or treating, which wasn't a bad idea.

Plain City Spooktacular, Henry typed in Century Gothic. *Come one, come all to an evening of horror, where murder and mayhem are the recipe of the day. Think Final Destination meets Texas Chainsaw Massacre. A night of blood-curdling screams that'll have you on the edge of your seats, the hair on the back of your necks charged, your hearts racing so fast that it'll crash out of your chest like Alien 1, 2, and 3 on steroids.*

Henry checked everything for errors, then sent it to Avery, whose computer dinged, indicating he got the article.

He gathered up his things and rose. He was going to go home and shower and change. Tonight might be the night he learned something important—something that could help find who murdered a woman so heinously. It'd be good to know that the person was in jail before the Halloween event. Because for some reason, this holiday brought out the crazies, and he hoped the person who murdered the victim in the barn wasn't one of them.

On the way to his car, he noticed Blake and Pastor Gabriel walking into the local print shop across the street. The two were together by how the man's hand lingered on the small of her back. That to Henry was an intimate gesture.

Why wouldn't they be a couple? She had heavenly eyes, and he worked for the man who lived there. Perfect fit. Henry, on the other hand, was one of the fallen—human weakness personified. Why would she ever want to be in the same room with him?

He stood on the street, his attention on the door. For some ungodly reason, he'd been drawn to her, and couldn't seem to shake it no matter how hard he tried. So unlike him. He'd never had an interest in any woman beyond sex, but Blake Allen was different. She made him want to get to know her, what she liked to do when she wasn't working. What kind of movies she watched? Silly, insignificant things he'd never thought about before. Why did she make him wonder? It was baffling, especially when she had no interest in him.

Maybe that was it. He wanted what he couldn't have kind of thing—made sense.

He dug into his pocket for his keys and unlocked the car door. He had to stop this obsession over her because it wouldn't get him anywhere. What he needed was a distraction. After all, it'd been months since he'd had any female companionship, eight months to be exact. Six of those he'd spent in house rehab and out-patient, longer than most, trying to figure out how to cope with what had happened. The last two, he'd been working his way back to the real world. Suppose some would call Plain City that. The small town wasn't his idea of real, but it was probably better that way. Real got him into trouble.

He glanced at the storefront again. Blake wasn't for him, and he might as well resign himself to that now. Besides, she was probably the type who'd want commitment, and Henry couldn't give her that. How could he? He wasn't staying here. As soon as he could, he planned to leave and go back to the life he knew—a life that made more sense to him. Plain City was a far reach from that.

****

Blake didn't know how she got wrangled into having dinner with Pastor Gabriel. It was all a big blur.

When he had come by the shop at closing time, he'd asked her to come along and pick out the new church's stationery. She was fine with that. Then, after they settled on a simple pattern with an elegant, easy to read font, he'd led her out the door, down the street, and straight into Connor's café. With no way of her saying no.

Gabriel pulled out her chair, and she sat, twisting her hands under the table. Everyone would see them together and assume they were dating, and she didn't want that. Rumors would run rampant. Words whispered from one person to the next, and by tomorrow, it would be the talk of the town. People would come into the coffee shop in the morning and ask questions—ones she'd be too uncomfortable to answer. If he'd brought sheet music along, that would be different. It'd look like they were discussing church business. Now, it appeared as if it were a date. The idea had her breathing shallowly.

"Would you two like coffee?" Frank Connor asked while he set two glasses of water on opposites sides of the large tissue-paper pumpkin in the middle of the table.

"Not for me." She glanced at Gabriel, who shook his head.

"Are you ready to order?"

"Give us a few minutes," Gabriel said with that reassuring smile of his that was supposed to make everyone feel at ease. Right now, it wasn't working for Blake. She quickly glanced around. Mark Griffith, the pharmacist, watched her intently, an irritating grin making matters worse. This whole thing was crazy. She was simply sharing a meal with the pastor of her church. Why was Blake so paranoid? She felt like a wound-up rubber band ready to snap.

"Do you know what you want?" Gabriel asked moments after she'd picked up the menu.

Blake's hands started to sweat, and she tried to concentrate on her choices, it all blurring together. Her skin began to prickle, her heart beating so fast that it threatened to leave her chest.

She swallowed hard and glanced around again, Susie Lichtin, a teller at the bank, staring daggers at her. Blake had no idea why. Suddenly, she felt like the walls were closing in on her.

"What are you going to have?" he asked again, forcing her to look at him. "I think I'll have the special."

She sucked in a labored breath. "Okay. That sounds good." Blake didn't even know what the special was, but she didn't care. Right now, she couldn't think straight. She'd give anything to be somewhere else.

Frank returned to take their order and left.

"I want to thank you again for helping me pick out the new stationery. I am so inept with that kind of stuff."

"No problem. I'm glad I could help." She shifted

uncomfortably in her chair and ran a finger under the collar of her T-shirt. She felt like she was suffocating.

The door to the café jingled, and Blake looked up to see Kiel step inside, dressed up in a crisp white shirt, gray trousers, and a blazer that matched. His hair seemed somewhat tamed.

And for some reason she couldn't look away. His presence strangely calmed her.

He hesitated only a moment when he saw them, then headed for the counter.

Frank walked into the kitchen and came back with a large lattice pie and handed it to Kiel. He handed the owner money, told him to keep the change, then left without a backward glance.

Where was he going? With a pie?

Jenell came to mind, and for whatever reason, it made her stomach tighten. Was it because of her friend? Or Kiel? Why had his presence comforted her when she was about to explode?

"What do you think of the new reporter?" Gabriel's question forced her attention back to him.

She swallowed again. "I'm not sure. I know we are supposed to look past people's failings, but it's hard for me when it's drug abuse." There was her past again, rearing its head. Was she ever going to get over it?

"We don't know what happened that led him down that dark path, Blake. But I understand your concern since he's dating Jenell."

"He isn't dating her," she snapped. Why, she had no idea.

"I'm sorry. I just assumed since the two were together at the social on Sunday."

"Just because they were together," she said, hoping

he'd get her meaning, "doesn't mean they're dating."

Their food arrived and ended the conversation, but not before she noticed the irises in his eyes darkening again. It was an indicator for him that he was angry but trying not to show it. Maybe she shouldn't have snapped at him. He didn't deserve that from her. She was so on edge, and she didn't know what she was doing.

All she wanted was to finish her meal and leave. She didn't feel well. She wanted to crawl into bed, pull the covers over her head, and go to sleep. Ever since she'd gone by Bev's, her dreams had been troubling visions of the older woman in tears, wailing. It had unnerved her. She hoped it was merely a dream. Yet, still, no one had heard from her, or Amy and Sarah, for that matter. In the history of Plain City, they'd had no one disappear without a trace. Now, they had three. The whole thing was bizarre.

"Are you all right, Blake? You haven't touched your food, and you look pale."

This was her way out. "No, I'm not feeling well, Gabriel. If you don't mind, I think I'll just go home?"

His eyes filled with concern—an emotion that made her feel worse. "Of course not. Would you like me to drive you?"

"No. I have my car at the shop. I'll be fine walking. You go ahead and finish your meal." She pulled out her wallet to pay for hers.

"I'll get it. It's the least I can do after your help today.

"Are you sure?"

"Absolutely," he said as she rose from her chair.

"Thanks, and I'll see you tomorrow night at church."

Blake didn't bother waiting for him to answer. She rushed to get out the door. She'd go get her car, then drive by Jenell's. If Kiel's car was there, then she'd know where he'd been going dressed to the nines. Maybe Pastor Gabriel was right. Perhaps the two were dating.

The idea alone didn't sit well. But it wasn't because of Henry. It had to be that Blake was worried for her best friend. Kiel had a checkered past, and she didn't want Jenell to be a casualty of that.

She unlocked the door of her car and was about to get in when someone from behind her grabbed her arm. Blake jumped back, then turned to find Amy, worry line etching the girl's forehead. "Oh my God," Blake cried. "Where have you been? Your mother is worried sick. I hope you've been home to see her."

Amy clutched her arm tighter and tugged her between the dumpster and the back wall of the coffee shop.

"I can't stay long. I have to tell you something."

"Okay," Blake said, unsure why the girl looked so scared. She was in the same clothes she'd been in the last time Blake had seen her, and her hair was matted and greasy. Where the heck had she been?

"You need to stay away—"

"Blake," Gabriel's voice echoed around the corner and made her turn.

When she looked back, Amy had disappeared.

What was going on?

The pastor walked toward her. "I wanted to make sure you made it to your car. You okay?"

"Yeah, I'm fine." She got into her SUV. She didn't want to hang around. She had too many questions and concerns about her employee. "I'll see you tomorrow."

The thing with Amy had freaked her out. What was the girl going to say to her? She wished Gabriel hadn't interrupted them.

Amy hadn't been home. Not the way she looked.

Blake turned onto Main Street. Sleep now would be virtually impossible after the encounter. Maybe she should go by the police station and talk to the sheriff. Tell him about seeing Amy and find out what he thought about the strange encounter. The girl looked frightened and didn't want anyone but Blake to see her. What could have terrified her so much?

Going by Jenell's was going to have to wait. This was more important. In Blake's gut, she knew Grandy had to be told about this, and right away.

****

Henry rang Jenell's doorbell, holding the pie he'd gotten from Connor's café in his other hand. She'd told him just to bring himself, but he wanted to come with something, and dessert seemed his best bet since alcohol was out of the question.

Off to the side of the porch, a black spider was strung on a fake web along with three carved pumpkins with glowing, fake candles that sat on a bale of straw. He glanced down the street and noticed that everyone seemed to have gotten into the holiday spirit. What would Christmas be like here? He could only imagine.

The door opened, and Jenell's face lit up with a bright smile.

He handed her the pie. "Hope you like apple."

"Love it, but you didn't have to."

Henry shrugged. "I know. I felt weird not bringing something."

"Come on in. We'll go to the kitchen, and I'll

introduce you to my mom."

He stepped inside and closed the door, then tailed her to the backside of the house. "Mom, I want you to meet Henry Kiel. Henry, this is my mom, Lillian."

He reached out and shook the older woman's hand, studying her face as he did. He instantly saw where Jenell had gotten her amber eyes and her fiery red hair.

"It's a pleasure to meet you, Henry. Jenell has been talking non-stop about you."

"Oh, I have not, Mom." A rosy glow moved up her neck and onto her cheeks.

"Okay, not non-stop, but she has mentioned you a time or two."

Henry smiled at Jenell, who looked as if she wanted to crawl under the table.

"Why don't you two go take a seat at the dining table, and I'll be right behind you."

"Henry brought a pie for dessert. Wasn't that nice?"

"Yes. Thank you."

Jenell placed it down on the counter and led him through an archway into a large room with stark white walls. There was a leafed table and a glass hutch that held stacks of blue and white antique dishes. The table had a light blue ruffled cloth and was set for three.

She pulled out one of the chairs for him and then sat. Henry joined her.

"How was your day at the newspaper? Any exciting news you can share?"

"Yeah, I got to write about our Halloween Spooktacular."

"Right. That's a big event here in Plain City. Everyone loves All Hallows Eve."

"I could tell by all the decorations."

She smiled again. "I know our town isn't what you're used to, but we do have our own charm."

"I can see that," he said, then smiled back at her.

"Here we go." Jenell's mother carried in two bowls of food—one filled with mashed potatoes, the other a cheesy broccoli and cauliflower mix. She left and returned with a plate of meat and a tray of dinner rolls. Everything looked and smelled delicious.

She sat down in the empty chair and handed him the pork chops.

Henry filled his plate and dug in. Jenell's mother was an excellent cook, and if he ate there long enough, he'd gain back every pound he'd lost the past two years and then some.

"Jenell said you used to work for the city and are still on the council. Would it be all right to ask you a few questions?"

"Of course. Jenell told me you are interested in the company who bought the old Linder place. Is that right?"

"Yes. Bolton Inc. I was wondering if you knew who was behind the name."

"That was what was strange. All the city got with their proposal was the name Bolton. When asked for more transparency, they backed away and decided not to utilize the land."

"But I thought they backed out because of a nosey reporter?"

"The city wanted it to seem that way. Blame him instead of the council. Malcolm Freemont did try to find out more about this group. Never really materialized since he just up and disappeared."

"And no one thought that was odd?"

"I believe your boss questioned what happened. The

man had worked at the *Tribune* for five years. If he hadn't left a letter at home, the sheriff would have investigated further."

Henry found this intriguing. "And he wrote the letter?"

"The man worked at the paper. It was typed and printed out."

He nodded, yet inside was screaming that anyone with a computer could have written the note. To him, that wasn't proof the man left Plain City on his own accord. Anything could have happened to him, perhaps by the same person who killed the victim in the barn.

"Would you like coffee and dessert now?" Jenell's mother asked, drawing his attention back to her.

"I'd love both."

Lillian's information had Henry's mind spinning, and his heart racing like it did when he was on a hot story overseas. This wasn't one vicious murder in a barn outside of town. Nope. It went way beyond that, and he intended to find out who Bolton Inc. represented and if they were willing to kill people to keep that hidden from plain sight.

Chapter Six

What was she doing here, sitting in the lobby of the police station? At this point, she wasn't even sure that what she saw was real. One second Amy was there, then she was gone. Poof. Like a mirage. Could lack of sleep have caused her to see things?

"Miss Allen." The sheriff walked toward her, a bright smile on his face. "You needed to see me?"

Blake sighed. She was going to tell him what happened and go from there. "I saw Amy for a moment today. I was getting in my car when she stopped me."

The man's brows drew together. "Had she been home to see her mother? Deana's been calling me every day, worried sick."

"I don't think she had. She was wearing the same clothes she'd been in the last day I saw her, and her hair looked awful like she hadn't washed it since. All she said was that she had to warn me about something. Pastor Gabriel interrupted, and she disappeared again. It was bizarre."

The sheriff shook his head. "That is strange. I'll call her mother and ask if she's home."

Blake nodded. "Maybe call Sarah's as well. Perhaps Theresa heard from her."

"I'll do that. Thanks for coming by."

"Anything from Beverly yet?" Blake asked.

He cleared his throat and shook his head. "Nothing."

Blake tightened the hold on her purse strap. "And you're not concerned about that?"

"Of course, I'm concerned, Blake. But right now, all we can do is wait and see. I'll keep you abreast if I find out anything."

"All right. Thanks, sheriff. Have a good evening."

"You, too."

Blake left the station. The whole trip had been a waste of time. The sheriff didn't seem to be taking any of this seriously, and that bothered her. She'd call Deana herself if she didn't think it'd make the woman worry more.

On the way to her car, she noticed Kiel across the street, still dressed up, parking in the visitor's area. Her car sat directly in front of the station.

What was he doing here?

She got into her vehicle and spied on him.

The sheriff stepped out of the building and met Kiel at the bottom of the steps. After a few moments, Kiel handed the sheriff a sheet of paper, shook his hand, then turned around and started back to his car.

Grandy glanced at the paper, then went back inside. Something was up with those two. This wasn't the first time she'd seen them talking. They'd been in a pow-wow during the church social, like the two had a private secret. Blake would love to know what that secret could be.

She revved the engine and pulled away from the curb. She planned to go home to shower then meet Jenell for their once a month Tuesday night bingo game at the Elks club. Saturdays they were weekly. She should stay home, but sleep would be elusive, and she hoped a few hours of laughing with her best friend would help.

Blake turned into her driveway and parked. Inside

her house, she padded down the hallway to the bedroom and leafed through her dresser drawers for something casual to wear. That done, she laid them on the bed and walked into the bathroom to turn on the shower, noting something missing from the sink. Where was her perfume? Had the bottle fallen?

She leaned down and moved the trashcan aside. No perfume. For as long as she'd lived in the house, she'd kept the bottle next to the sink. Where was it? Maybe she'd accidentally thrown it out. It had to be something as simple as that.

Blake sighed, then stripped out of her clothes and stepped into the shower, the warm spray hitting her square in the chest. Hopefully, by the time she washed up and had gotten dressed, she'd feel more herself.

An hour later, she entered the Elks club, the smell of popcorn making her stomach growl since she hadn't touched her food from earlier. She'd have to get some to snack on. She quickly paid for her Bingo cards, grabbed a tub of popcorn and coffee, then found a seat. Jenell wasn't there yet.

She laid her cards out, opened the red marker, and munched on her corn, glancing around the room. Her heart stopped when she saw Pastor Gabriel standing by the door, his eyes on her.

Crap. Blake had told him she was going home, that she wasn't feeling well. Now, she looked like a liar. And he didn't appear to be happy about that.

What was he doing here? He'd never come before.

She turned away and pretended to study her cards. Minutes ticked by, and sweat coated the back of her white, cotton T-shirt.

"What's with you?" her best friend asked, startling

Blake and forcing her to look up.

"What do you mean?"

"Are you hoping to will your numbers to be called by staring at them?"

Blake gave her a crooked smile. "Of course not. I'm just…"

"Did you see Pastor Gabriel's here?"

"Yes. I'm avoiding him."

Jenell plopped down next to her. "What? Why?"

"I was with him earlier at the cafe, and I told him I wasn't feeling well. Now, he probably thinks I'm a liar."

"I don't understand. I thought you liked Gabriel."

"I do like him. But I get the feeling he might want something more, and you know how I am about dating."

"Oh my God, Blake, did he ask you out?"

"Sort of, yes."

"And you said no? Are you crazy? Gabriel Huntington is the best-looking guy in town. No, wait, Henry has that honor, but he's a close second. You need to get over your fears. Gabriel is a grown man, not a teenage boy."

"You think Henry Kiel is better looking than Gabriel?" Blake stared at her friend.

"Of course, he is. You should have seen him earlier today all dressed up. His olive skin in total contrast to a crisp, bright white shirt. So damned hot. I think he might like me, too."

"I saw him. He came into Connor's to pick up a pie while Gabriel and I were there. Did he have dinner with you?"

"Mom and me, yeah. He had questions he wanted to ask her."

Blake scrunched her brow. "What kind of

questions?"

"Who was behind Bolton Inc., among other things."

She shifted in the metal chair. "Why is Henry so interested in that company? Is he writing a story about them or something?"

Jenell shrugged. "He didn't say, and I didn't ask."

A loud voice crackled across the intercom. "Thanks for coming this evening. Let's get started. The first pot you are all playing for is sixty dollars. Good luck, everyone."

Blake forced herself to focus on the game. If Gabriel came up and asked if she was feeling better, she'd simply say yes. If he didn't believe her, then that was something he'd have to deal with. She respected the man as pastor of their church, but she didn't like the way she'd gotten railroaded into having a meal with him. The sooner he understood she didn't want to see him in that capacity, the better it was for them both. Yes, she needed to work out her past, but she wasn't ready to do that now.

****

Henry sat in his cubicle, staring at his computer screen as he typed in Malcolm Freemont's name, hoping the man had a recent article somewhere. He needed to talk to the guy. There was some reason the reporter was looking into Bolton, and Henry wanted to know what that could have been.

On the search engine, three different Freemont's came up. One was from New York City. Another from Oakland, California. The last was from Arkansas. He clicked on the name and found some of his stories from the *Tribune* and all the guy's social media pages. He clicked on Facebook and noticed no new posts. He found the same on his Twitter and Instagram accounts. "Damn it all to hell." Where did the man disappear to? A reporter with no new bylines was dead in this business. Henry knew that all too well. *But did that mean*... maybe he was in a whole new line of work now, or simply went off the grid.

"Hey," Simon said, coming up behind him. "Everyone is saying that they loved your Halloween piece. That it was clever, while informative. Good work."

"Thanks. I appreciate that."

"How's that story coming along you promised me a week or two ago?"

Shit. Here we go again. After a week and a half, Henry didn't have anything new. "No one is willing to commit to anything on the record."

Simon's lips thinned out into a straight line. "You can't tell me anything at all about what it entails? I mean, come on, Kiel. It's starting to sound like you've made this story up."

Henry understood his editor's frustration. He felt it too. "I'm telling you the truth, Simon. I wish I could reveal everything, but I promised my source I wouldn't until they gave me the green light."

"All right. I've got something else I want you to work on until that comes through. Rumor has it that the Fellowship church has tripled in size the last six months and is getting looked at for a televised broadcast. All because of the pastor, Gabriel Huntington. I want to know what it is about him that has drawn so many to his congregation. I want an in-depth look at the man himself. Do you think you can do that?"

"Of course," Henry said, not all that excited about the concept. After all, the guy had managed to attract the one woman Henry had found intriguing, a female who looked at him as if he was the lowest form of amoeba. But Simon wanted him on the story, and he wouldn't let him down. He'd be so thorough that everyone who read the article would know the man inside and out. "I'll get right on it."

He gathered the things he'd need and rose. Hopefully, the pastor wouldn't have a problem talking with him.

Henry would have to tread lightly. The best way to get a story like this was to mirror the man for a few days—creating a day in the pastor's life. Those type of rigorous interviews were always received well. At least the ones he'd done.

Outside, heavy rain had him racing for his car. By the time he jumped inside and was on the road, his hair dripped onto his face and chilled him to the bone. He needed a cup of coffee to warm him up. He'd stop into Allen's and get some. Simon had been right that Blake Allen made the best in town, not to mention being the prettiest thing behind a counter. Just thinking about her had his heart skittering crazily in his chest.

Henry hadn't seen her since rushing into Connor's restaurant to pick up the pie he'd ordered—another man Henry needed to interview soon. Blake had been with the pastor, yet her expression suggested she hadn't been all that thrilled. Although, that could have been from seeing him.

A few minutes into his commute, he parked in front of the coffee shop. Henry stepped inside, surprised to find it empty. He didn't even see Blake. "Hello. Anybody here?"

Blake came out from the back, her skin ashen, dark

circles under her eyes.

"You okay?" Instinctively, he wanted to reach out and touch her arm but thought better of it.

"Just feeling a little under the weather. I guess there must be a bug going around."

"Maybe you should close and go home and rest. I could help if you'd like."

"You're probably right. I don't want to get anyone else sick." Blake wiped at her sweaty brow. "This has never happened to me before. I thought I could work through it. I was lucky that business was slow today."

"Is there anything I could do to help you get out of here sooner?" Henry asked. "I'm in no hurry to be anywhere."

"I wouldn't want to—"

"Let me help," he said, cutting her off.

"I was trying to finish up the dishes and put everything away in the walk-in."

"Great. Let's do that so you can get home. I'll put the sign up and lock the door. I'll meet you back there."

She hesitated, then turned and left.

Henry rushed to close. He didn't care that he was supposed to be on his way to the church. Blake needed his help, and that was all that mattered now.

He took over loading everything she told him to into the big freezer, then washed the remaining dishes while she dried them. An hour later, she led him out the back door and secured the lock. "Thank you again, Mr. Kiel. I appreciate the help."

"No problem, and please call me Henry."

"Okay, thanks, Henry. I better get home." She opened her car door.

"Tell Jenell hello for me," Henry said, leaning into

the car door.

"You two don't have a date tonight?"

"We're not dating." Had her friend suggested they were? Had he given her that impression? *God.* Maybe he had.

Her incredible green eyes widened. "I just assumed that you were."

"Would it be an assumption for me to suggest that you and Pastor Gabriel are an item?"

"That would be a false assumption. Could we continue this discussion another time? I'm not feeling well."

"Of course. Are you sure you can drive home? I could give you a lift."

"I'm okay. Thanks again."

Henry watched her pull out of the back then walked around the side of the building, catching sight of a black sedan that pulled in behind Blake's car. Was it a coincidence, or had someone been watching, waiting for her to leave? Henry had to be sure.

He jumped behind the wheel of his car and spun around to catch up with the convoy. He tailed at a distance, not wanting them to see him. Every time Blake made a turn, the sedan mirrored the move. By the time she parked in front of a two-story brick home, he was confident that whoever was in the car was indeed following her. But why?

Right before making the turn onto Champion Drive, Henry pulled his car to the curb. The sedan drove past Blake as she stepped inside her front door, then parked a few houses down.

How could he, in good faith, leave knowing someone was watching her? The person could be a rapist or a killer. They had someone in town capable of ripping a body in two. No way was he going to let that happen to Blake.

But what was he going to do? Walk up and ring her bell? She'd think *he* was a stalker. Calling the sheriff might give Grandy more ammunition to use against him. He could hear it now. *"Why were you following Miss Allen?"* The sheriff didn't think much of him or what he'd managed to dig up on Bolton.

Henry's only option now was to jot down the plate number, then sit back and wait. If anyone got within a foot of her house, he'd be there to find out why.

He blew out a deep breath.

Maybe he could casually walk by the car—see who was inside? Yet perhaps that'd spook them. He didn't want to do that unless he had to.

Nope. Henry would sit here and watch.

What he wouldn't give for a cup of Blake's coffee right about now. But she had already placed the pots in the sink, ready to wash. So, he'd have to slog through without caffeine and hope the car left before he nodded out from lack of sleep and boredom.

Chapter Seven

Blake opened her eyes only to have everything in the room tilt sideways. What was wrong with her? The dizziness in her head made her stomach churn.

The day before, she'd gotten up, showered, her regular routine before leaving for work. An hour in, her stomach started to ache, then her head began to pound against her skull like nothing she'd ever experienced before. She'd had to force herself to get through most of the day until Henry came in around two. By then, she was struggling to keep anything down, which wasn't much. Barely a sip of her favorite Earl Grey tea and a few bites of dry toast.

Henry's offered help was utterly unexpected yet very much appreciated. She wasn't sure if she would have been able to do it all on her own. The man was not who she had first thought. He acted genuinely concerned about her welfare. That shocked her and had her looking at him in a new light. And with that enlightenment, she'd come to realize Jenell was right. Henry Kiel was strikingly handsome. Maybe a little too thin, but still nice on the eyes.

Blake eased to her side and tried to slide off the bed, her focus spinning around in circles. By the time she'd made it to the bathroom, she knew she was going to vomit. All she could think was she'd contracted a flu bug from someone, but she couldn't remember anyone around her saying they'd been ill.

If she could get to the doctor, she'd go in. Too bad she couldn't even get out of the bathroom. After her stomach settled, she lay on the cold floor, wishing she hadn't gotten out of bed. She felt like a ragdoll, unable to move.

Her cell phone started ringing on her nightstand in the bedroom, but Blake was too weak to get to it. She closed her eyes, only to have strange images twinkling behind her lids. Red and yellow flashes of color that hurt her forehead even more. An odd vibration coursed through her body, a tingling sensation that started at the top of her skull and moved to the tips of her toes. She tried to open her eyes again but couldn't. With each labored breath she took, her heart rate jumped. Then it became hard to breathe at all as her throat tightened.

What if this was what it felt like to be dying?

The knocking at the door had her struggling again to get up, yet no matter how hard she tried, she couldn't move. It was as if she were paralyzed. Before now, she'd never been sick a day in her life, and here she lay wondering if she'd ever see her friends and family again. God help her.

Her head began to swim, and she found herself feeling weightless.

"Blake," Jenell's voice called from what seemed like a mile away. "Can you hear me, sweetie?"

Then, she heard her friend talking to someone.

"You have to wake up, Blake." Jenell touched her cheek lightly, and Blake tried again to open her eyes, managing to crack them halfway. "Honey, what's wrong? Can you tell me what happened?"

She blinked, attempting to talk, but her mouth was

too dry.

"Hang in there. Help's coming."

Henry? Was he going to come see her? She hoped she could keep her eyes open long enough to see him. Feet shuffling had her turning her head, hoping it was him. It wasn't. Two men in dark blue uniforms rushed into the room, one holding a red bag. "What's going on?" the youngest of the two asked, looking at Blake, then to Jenell.

"I don't know. I found her here on the bathroom floor. I can't get her to respond to anything besides opening her eyes."

"Step back and let us take a look," the other said, leaning down and flashing light in Blake's eyes. "Her pupils are responsive." He then placed something on her arm and a cold instrument on her chest.

Blake closed her eyes, and the strange patterns returned, almost like dancing fire behind her lids—something she'd never seen in her life. Whatever the vision was, she hoped it would stop. The yellow flames built in intensity, and images of figures appeared—and as they moved closer, she recognized two. Who the people were had her sucking in a huge breath, then everything went black.

****

Henry stared in shock at the ambulance, lights flashing, parked outside Blake's house. Jenell's car sat directly in front of it. *Oh, Jesus Christ.*

Why hadn't he stayed?

The sedan from the night before had left forty-five minutes into his vigil, which gave him no reason to remain. Had they seen him and left, then come back when he'd gone?

Damn it all to hell. He should have stayed all night.

He quickly parked across the street and exited his car. If she was seriously hurt, he'd never forgive himself. One death at his hands was enough.

The door to her home was wide open as he raced inside. He rushed from one room to the next, finding two paramedics and Jenell hovering over Blake in the bathroom.

Jenell looked up, tears clouding her eyes, eyes that widened when she saw him.

"I was driving by and saw the lights. What's going on?"

She ran into his arms and sobbed. Henry held her tight, feeling entirely out of his depth. A crying female was worse than ducking heavy gunfire. Hell, he'd rather take a hit.

"What's wrong with her?" he asked one of the EMTs?"

"I'm not sure. The woman has a weak heart rate, but other than that, I don't know. I think we should transfer her to the hospital, so that they can run some tests."

"I'm going with her," Jenell said, wiping at her tears. "I'll call her family on the way to the hospital."

Henry wished he could go too. The thought of her death made his gut hurt. He needed to know she'd recover. "Would you like me to come and wait with you? That way, you'll have a ride back to get your car."

She clasped his arm. "Would you do that?"

"Of course. I'll be right behind you."

He followed Jenell and the gurney out and closed the door. He shouldn't be doing this. He had a story to write. But he needed to know that Blake was going to be okay before he met with Pastor Gabriel. Simon would have to wait a day or so longer. Hopefully, he could live with that. If not, Henry would be looking for another job.

Twenty minutes into the ride, Henry entered the hospital emergency parking area. He locked his car doors and walked in, the smell of antiseptic instantly turning his stomach. He remembered the odor, and how he'd spent days in the hospital after the explosion with a hip fracture and concussion. The whole time feeling crushed from the loss of Maverick.

Henry shook his head and moved down the long hallway to Jenell, who paced in front of the nurse's stations, her arms wrapped protectively around her waist.

Henry inhaled a breath, wondering if the doctors had looked at Blake yet. When Jenell saw him, she ran to him again, flinging her arms around him.

"She'll be okay. Did you call her family?"

She looked up at him, her eyes glassy with tears. "Yes. They're on their way."

"Good. Now, let's you and I go grab some coffee. We might be here a while."

She shook her head. "I don't want to leave in case the doctor comes out to tell me something."

"All right. I'll go get us a cup. You sit down." He led her to a chair and waited until she sat. "How do you like your coffee?"

"With cream and sugar."

"Okay, I'll be right back.

Henry took off down the hallway, following the arrows that pointed the way to the café.

As he headed back with two cups of coffee in his hand, he ran into Pastor Gabriel, who was on his way to the nurse's station. He looked surprised to see Henry.

"Are you here with Jenell?"

"Yes. How did you hear about Miss Allen?"

"Blake's neighbor is one of our parishioners. She called to tell me that she was brought by ambulance to the hospital. I rushed down here to see how she was doing. Have you heard anything yet?"

"No. I went to get coffee for Jenell."

The man nodded. "Do you mind if I wait with you two?"

For some reason, Henry wanted to say, yes, he did, but how charitable would that be? It was a free country. He didn't get to say who stayed or went. Gabriel could do what he liked. This might be an opportunity to get some preliminaries on the man and ask if he could do that story Simon wanted him to do.

"Not at all. Blake needs all the support she can get."

"Pastor Gabriel." Jenell rose from her chair. "It was so good of you to come."

Gabriel rubbed Jenell's arm. "Cheryl Perkins called me. I had to promise to keep her up to date on Blake. Have you been told anything yet?" The concern on the pastor's face turned Henry's stomach. He cared about Blake.

"Only that she's stable," Jenell said, drawing Henry away from the man. "They ran some bloodwork. It could take an hour or so to come back."

Henry handed Jenell her coffee.

Thanks." She took a sip. "I hope to go in and see her soon."

"Let's all take a seat," Gabriel said, then sat in the last chair against the wall. "Did anyone call Blake's parents?"

"Yeah. They are on their way."

"Am I right that they live in Little Rock?"

"Yes. It might be a while before the two get here."

Henry sat on the other side of Jenell and sipped his coffee, suddenly feeling like the odd man out. These people had a history with Blake. He knew absolutely nothing about her besides the fact that she had the most intense green eyes that cut right to his soul—eyes that drew him in the moment he saw her. That, and she worked hard and didn't mince words with him. He respected that about her.

Out of the corner of his eye, he noticed a young lady with long, dark hair peeking around the corner, down the hall where he'd turned to get coffee. Her attention seemed glued to the pastor. When she saw Henry looking, she stepped back and disappeared. What the hell was that about? Was she waiting for Gabriel?

What was it about the man that seemed to evoke such adoration from the female gender?

Henry glanced over at him. Okay, so he had charisma and an air of authority about him. Was that enough to attract people to his congregation—draw them in to hear him preach? Henry didn't know. Maybe he'd have to go to church services one of these Sundays to find out.

"So, pastor, I've heard great things about your guidance at Christian Fellowship. Can you tell me the secret to your success?" Henry asked.

The pastor smiled. "I don't think I have a 'secret'. I simply try to be open to the people who walk through those church doors. Welcome them with open arms and listen to their problems. I don't think that's anything but good fellowship. Hardly a secret formula of any kind."

Henry wanted to roll his eyes but thought better of it. Was he being petty because of the pastor's connection to Blake, or was it something else in the man's gestures that bugged him? He wasn't sure.

Gabriel frowned. "Why do you ask?"

"My editor has been hearing good things about you and was hoping you'd be willing to talk to the *Tribune* about your work."

The man shifted in his seat. Was he uncomfortable with the idea? It seemed like it to Henry. "It would be completely on your terms, and you could have last say on the piece before it went to print."

"I'm flattered, but I'm not here to feather my cap. This is about bringing people to God. That's not worth praising to me. It's my job."

"I understand that. I only ask that you take a day or two to think about it."

"All right. Just don't get your hopes up. I'm private. Having a story written about me goes against who I am. What brought me to Plain City."

"Who's here for Blake Allen?" a thin man in scrubs asked, drawing all three of them to him.

"I'm her best friend. Her parents are on their way." Jenell jumped up from her seat.

"We are still waiting on the bloodwork, but she is conscious and talking now. She was extremely dehydrated, and we are flushing her with fluids. Her vitals are normal at this point. I think we will be keeping her overnight, but she'll probably go home in the morning if all the tests come back normal."

Jenell leaned into Henry and heaved a sigh.

"Thank you, doctor." Gabriel shook the man's hand. "Can we go in and see her?"

"Yes, but only two at a time."

"Okay. Thanks again."

The doctor turned and walked back down the hall.

"You and Gabriel go ahead and see her. I need to call work anyway." Henry wanted to see Blake, yet he had no right to. He certainly wasn't family or a friend. He was a man she barely tolerated, not unlike his parents, who didn't even want him around when they were dealing with an illness. Henry was sure Blake wouldn't either.

Henry walked down the hall, removing his phone from his pocket. Suddenly he needed to know how his mother was doing. This experience had taught him something important. Life was short, and he should stop being petty and foolish.

He scrolled through his numbers and found his sister's, and pressed call. It immediately sent him to her voicemail. Should he leave a message? If he did, would she get back to him? Only one way to find out. Henry left a brief message and asked her to please return his call when she could. Either she would or she wouldn't. The ball was now in Karen's court, and one way or the other, he'd accept it.

Chapter Eight

"No, Mom, I think I can do it." Blake had never experienced such a feeling of helplessness. She'd been home from the hospital for three days now, and her parents still refused to let her get out of bed. "Don't get me wrong. I love having you here. It's just that if I don't get up and move around, I'm going to go crazy."

"All right, sweetheart, but you must promise you won't over-do and send yourself back to the ER. We still don't know what happened to cause your collapse."

Blake crossed a finger over her heart. "I promise."

Her mother looked skeptical yet stepped away from the bed.

This was Blake's chance. She wasn't going to wait for her mother to change her mind. She shoved the covers aside and stood, grabbing hold of the edge of the nightstand when she lost her balance. Was she ever going to feel one hundred percent again? Even fifty percent at this point would be good.

Her doctor had told her that something strange came back in her bloodwork. Yet, they couldn't isolate what it was, or even if it was the cause of her illness. All they could say for sure was her blood sugar levels were very low, without being an insulin issue, and she was taking high doses of vitamin B6 to counteract whatever it was.

"Do you need me to help you to the bathroom?" Her mother hovered next to her again.

"No, I'm fine. I have to regain my strength, and the only way to do that is to walk on my own." Her bravado was probably going to be Blake's downfall. She should allow her mom to help, but at this point, she refused to backpedal. Slowly, she shuffled across the floor to the door of the bathroom, clutching the frame for a moment to catch her breath. Feeling like this was foreign to her. Blake had always had more energy than most people. This seriously sucked.

She inhaled a breath, then blew it out, frustrated to no end. Her legs felt like Jell-O. So, a shower was out of the question since she'd have to remain standing. Taking a bath would be better if she could manage to get in and out of the tub.

Blake leaned down and turned on both faucets and poured in some bath salts. She eased out of her pajamas and climbed into the tub, the hot water encircling her body.

She sighed with contentment. Sponge baths were nothing compared to this.

Her head instinctively lolled back against the rim of the tub, the scent of the lavender and chamomile soothing her into complacency. She closed her eyes, and images of Henry Kiel appeared. Blake quickly reopened them.

What the heck was wrong with her? Why had he come to mind? Was it because he'd helped her the day before she'd gone to the hospital? Or the fact that he'd waited with Jenell to learn if she was okay. Blake didn't know. He was kind and caring. So unlike what she'd first thought about him.

When the water started to cool, she washed her hair and body, then reached for a towel and got out. Her breathing labored, and her heartrate picked up. It pissed her off that simple tasks wore her out. By the time she was dressed and had dried her hair as best she could, she was ready to go back to bed, but refused to do so. She had a business to run. She couldn't keep Allen's closed forever. She had to get better so she could go back to work.

"Do you feel up to going downstairs to have some breakfast?" Her mom studied her closely.

"Yes. I'll follow you."

Her mother's green eyes narrowed. "Are you sure?"

"Yes, I'm good, Mom." If Blake kept this up, she might win an award for the biggest lie she'd ever told. An Oscar nod, perhaps.

When her foot hit the landing on the ground floor, her energy fed on her triumph. Once in the kitchen, she smiled, happy she'd forced herself into making the trek.

"What do you feel hungry for this morning?" Her mother looked inside the refrigerator. "I'm going to have to go to the store later. All you have are eggs. How about an omelet?"

"Sounds good."

Blake walked to the coffeemaker and poured a cup of coffee. Usually, she didn't have coffee at home since she could get some at work.

She sat at the table. Having her mom here was comforting. It had been six months since her parents had moved to the capital to be near her youngest sister, who had just had their first grandchild. Blake really couldn't blame them, yet she missed having them close by.

"How's Kayla doing?"

Her mother turned from the stove. "Your sister's fine. A little tired from Braden not sleeping much. But she couldn't be happier."

"How does Dad like the new house? Is he finding things to keep him busy?"

"You know your father. If he's not in the garden, he's working in the garage building something. He's got a whole new canvas to work with now."

Blake took a sip of her coffee, wishing she could step outside and get some crisp, fall air. This was her favorite time of the year, and here she was stuck inside the house. Hopefully, she'd have enough energy to have trick-or-treaters this year.

Her mother set a plate in front of her and another for herself, then rushed to get some silverware and a cup of coffee.

Once she had a fork in hand, Blake dug into her food. The sooner she built up her strength, the sooner she'd be well enough to go outside and start living her life again. For the past three days, her mind had been spinning worst-case scenarios about what was wrong with her. But all that did was make her feel sick. Worrying wouldn't help her at all. Maybe she'd never know what happened. A baffling diagnosis, the ones they did stories about on television. But as long as it didn't happen again, she was going to try and put it behind her.

The doorbell ringing had her trying with little success to get up.

"I'll get it." Her mother nudged her back into her chair.

Blake complied. Not that she had a choice.

Seconds later, her mother returned with Jenell in tow.

"You're up. How are you feeling?" Her best friend plopped down into one of the empty chairs.

"I'm still weak, but I'm getting there."

"Are you taking your medication?"

Blake smirked. "Like Mom would let me get away with that."

Jenell smiled. "How's she been as a patient? She's not giving you a hard time, is she?"

"You know Blake."

Blake drummed her fingers on the table. "Hey, I've been a model patient."

"Oh." Jenell reached for something in her purse. "I forgot to give you this yesterday." She handed her a white envelope. "Gabriel asked me to give it to you."

Blake stared at her name printed on the front. Reluctantly, she slid the card from inside that read, *Get Well Soon.*

She opened it and read the lovely sentiments. Blake should feel something here, but since their forced dinner date and the look he'd given her at the Elks, her gut told her to steer clear of him in an overly friendly way. She was afraid he'd expect more, and she wasn't ready for anything like that. She wondered if she'd ever be ready. Probably not with him. No matter how handsome and charismatic he was.

She closed the card. "Tell the pastor thank you."

Both Jenell and her mother's eyes narrowed. "That's it?" Jenell grabbed for the card. "I think he was hoping you'd invite him over to see you."

"I'm not up to having visitors yet." Blake hoped that the admission would be enough to get Jenell to drop the subject. Inviting Gabriel Huntington to her house wasn't something she felt comfortable doing, especially in her weakened state. Yet, Blake didn't want to come out and say that. Her best friend might blab it to someone who'd whisper to another person, and then she'd learn, the whole town knew, including the pastor. That would be the biggest nightmare ever.

****

Henry pressed the Fellowship church number into his cell phone and waited. Pastor Gabriel still hadn't gotten back to him on the story the paper wanted to run. He hoped the man had simply been too busy, and that's why he hadn't called.

The phone rang and rang and rang. Henry clicked end and tossed it onto the desk. Without Gabriel's permission, there wasn't much Henry could do, unless he went another route and talked to members of the church instead. At least until Henry was able to get Gabriel to relent, he could speak to Jenell. Maybe her boss. The couple from the hardware store. *And Blake.* Just thinking about her gave him a charge of adrenaline.

He sighed, then looked around the newsroom. Right now, he'd do some preliminary work on Gabriel Huntington. Like where he'd worked before coming to Plain City.

On his keyboard, he brought up the search engine and typed in the guy's name. Nothing came up. Maybe he spelled it wrong. He tried spelling it a different way. Still nothing. That was strange. He'd try something else. He typed in the church, and Pastor Ames came up. He clicked on the link and was able to get a number to reach the man, which was local. Henry grabbed his phone again and punched in the number. After the third ring, a man answered. "Pastor Ames?" Henry held his breath, hoping this wasn't a wild goose chase.

"I was. Who's asking?"

"I'm Henry Kiel. I work at the *Tribune*. I was hoping

83

to meet with you to talk about you retiring from the church."

"What do you want to know?"

"I'd like to meet with you in person to talk. Would that be possible?"

"Okay. When and where?"

Henry glanced at his watch. It was already eleven-thirty. "How about Connor's later this afternoon? Whatever time works best for you."

Good. Finally, something was going Henry's way.

"Any time after three would be fine," the pastor said.

"So, three-thirty at Connor's?"

"Sure, that would be good."

"Okay. See you then."

Henry ended the call and leaned back in his chair. He needed to prepare for the meeting—had to make a list of questions to ask. It might be his only chance, and he wasn't going to waste his time. Henry hoped Pastor Ames could tell him something about Gabriel that could help send him in the right direction. Then, he'd talk to members of the church.

By the time he had his list made, it was time for lunch. He grabbed his phone and tablet, unsure if he'd come back before he met up with the pastor.

In his car and on the road, Henry debated on where to go to eat. If Allen's were open, he'd love to go by and see how Blake was doing. But according to Simon, the coffee shop was still closed. How was she doing now? He'd love to know. Maybe he could ask Jenell when he talked to her.

The last time he'd seen Blake, she was lying on her bathroom floor. The whole event had kicked him hard in the gut. And to have heard that the doctors weren't sure what had caused her episode was unsettling. Could it happen again? Was there an underlying issue that Blake didn't know about?

He had to stop obsessing over a woman who probably thought he was a waste of space.

The Dairy Freeze sign caught his attention. A burger and shake sounded good.

He pulled in to park. As he was walking to the door, someone behind him called his name. He turned to find Sheriff Grandy headed toward him.

"Sheriff. What's up?"

"I was going in to have lunch. Care to join me."

"Sure." Henry still hadn't learned anything about the victim in the barn, and he'd relayed all the info he'd found on Bolton Inc. to him. Hopefully, this was merely an offer to enjoy a meal together.

Once they got their food, they sat in a booth in the back, far away from the restaurant's other people.

Henry was going to sit and eat. He'd let Grandy ask the questions—if he had any.

The older man took a drink of his shake, then looked at Henry, the deep V in his forehead suggesting the man had been dealing with a lot.

"I'm going to tell you something that's between you and me, Kiel. I can trust that it will remain that way, right?"

"Of course."

"Okay. Those two girls I told you about at the social are still missing. One of them works for Blake Allen. The other is that girl's best friend. They've been missing for over a week now. The only person who has seen one is Blake. Amy grabbed her behind the coffeehouse the day before Blake collapsed, but she quickly disappeared when someone interrupted them."

"Did Blake tell you about this meeting?"

"Yes. Blake came by right after it happened. She thought I should know. I called Amy's mother to see if she'd heard from her, but she said she hadn't. She was alive last Tuesday when Blake saw her. This whole thing has me more than concerned. Why are these girls hiding from their families? It just doesn't make sense."

"Does anything in this town?"

"Look, Kiel, nothing like this has ever happened before in Plain City. Right now, they are considered runaways and eighteen. They're adults. There's not a lot I can do."

"Do you have pictures of these girls? I could keep an eye out for them."

The sheriff reached into his breast pocket and pulled out some pictures and handed them to Henry. The snapshot on top was a young blonde. He'd never seen her, and he was good with faces. He flipped to the next and did a double take. It was the girl from the hospital. The one he thought was watching Pastor Gabriel.

Henry turned the picture toward the sheriff. "I saw her at the hospital when Blake was admitted."

Grandy's eyes widened. "Are you sure?"

"Yes. The girl was peeking around the corner at us." "Us?"

"Me, Jenell, and Pastor Gabriel. We were waiting to hear something on Blake."

The sheriff frowned. "Why do you think she was watching you?"

"I don't think she was watching all of us. I think she was spying on the pastor."

"The pastor. Why do you think that?"

Henry tapped the picture on the table. "Because her eyes were glued to him. When she saw that I was looking at her, she took off. I didn't see her again. I got the feeling she might have been there with him. Though, I could be wrong."

The sheriff rubbed at his chin. "That's weird since Blake told me Amy took off when the pastor showed up. This is something I'm going to investigate. A direction to explore. Thanks for the lead."

Henry took a bite of his burger. He wasn't sure if he was telling Grandy this because it could help in his investigation or somehow try to get back at Gabriel for not calling him. Either way, if it helped the sheriff find these missing women, that's all that mattered?

He and Grandy finished their meal and then went their separate ways.

Two hours later, after checking in at the paper, Henry headed for Connor's to meet Pastor Ames. He wanted to learn something about the man who now ran the Christian Fellowship church. Hopefully, the older pastor would be able to tell Henry something.

Inside the café, he glanced around and noted an older, balding man sitting alone at the counter. He made his way over to him, struck by the calm Henry felt as he neared him. Just the opposite of what he'd felt around Gabriel. Was there something there, or was it just jealousy about Blake? Henry wasn't sure.

"Pastor Ames?" He reached out his hand.

The man smiled. "Yes. Are you Henry?"

"I am. Could we go sit at that back booth?"

"I don't see why not." The older man slid off the stool and followed Henry away from everyone else. Henry didn't need an audience right now—one that might warn Gabriel of their talk.

The waitress brought a pot of coffee and filled their cups, then left.

"So, what did you want to know about the Fellowship church?" the pastor asked, then took a sip of his coffee.

"How long were you pastor there, and why did you decide to retire?"

"It was time. Pastor Gabriel came along at the perfect moment. I was thankful to turn over the reins to him."

"Really? Why's that?"

"I couldn't give the members the time they needed. Gabriel is young and vital. Has done a fantastic job of growing the church in the short time he's been there."

"How did you come to hire him?"

The older man sighed. "I got a call from him about a year ago. He was looking for a new church to apprentice at and wanted to work with me. He helped for the months leading up to my retirement. Then took over."

"What do you think of him?" Henry watched him closely.

"He's hands-on, with a force I've never seen before."

"How do you mean?"

"He breezed through a room like a blast of cold air, yet people flocked to him. It was the reason I thought it best to let go of the reins."

Henry could relate to the chilly feeling. He'd gotten that from Gabriel every time he'd been around him.

"But you have no idea where he'd been before coming to Plain City?"

"He showed me the papers of where he'd gone for his Seminary. I assumed he'd just finished his studies," the man said, suddenly looking annoyed. "But I thought this meeting was about my retirement. Not about Gabriel."

"It is," Henry lied, feeling a little guilty about the ruse. "Now, tell me about how you started and how you got here."

Chapter Nine

Blake flipped on the light and looked around the coffee shop, excited to be back at work. After a week of being home, lying around, she'd finally felt well enough to reopen, with help from her mother. Her dad had gone to Little Rock the day before and would be back in a few days when Blake was strong enough to run things on her own again.

"Where do we start?" her mother asked, then grabbed an apron and wrapped it around her waist.

"We're probably going to have to throw everything out and start from scratch."

Her mother nodded. "Are you sure you're up for this?"

"Yes." Blake reached for another apron and put it on. "I need to get back to work."

"Okay. If you're sure."

"I love that you're concerned, Mom, but I'm good. I promise."

They tossed out old product for forty-five minutes, washing everything that it was in up, and readied the dough for rising. Blake blew out a breath and wiped at her brow. She still had so much to do before opening at eight.

She left the kitchen to start a pot of coffee. She needed a jolt of caffeine before attempting the next hour of work.

"Do these turnovers look okay?" her mother asked when Blake returned, in her hands two cups of her favorite roast.

"They are perfect. How could they not be? You taught me everything I know."

Her mother slid the tray into the rack and grasped the mug she held out. "You've had a lot more practice than I have."

Blake smiled. That was true, but her mother was a perfectionist, and she wasn't worried about any pastries made by her hands.

Three hours from start to finish, everything was ready and in the bakery case.

Blake switched on the open sign and unlocked the door. She'd expect it to be slow the first couple of days until people realized she had opened up again.

When she'd made it back to the counter, the door jingled. She turned around to see Henry—the one man she'd been thinking a lot about the last week. Seeing him made her heart skip a much-needed beat, then proceeded to run a marathon in her chest, a reaction so foreign to her.

"Good morning." Henry's eyes connected with hers.

Blake swallowed hard. "Hi."

He walked to the counter, the scent of pine and exotic spices wafting in her direction. Why hadn't she ever noticed how nice he smelled before or how compelling his large, liquid brown eyes were—hooded by the longest, sootiest lashes she'd ever seen on a man. They were simply intoxicating.

"How are you feeling?" he asked, smiling.

Blake's eyes diverted to his mouth. It was damned nice, too.

"Blake? Are you okay?"

She cleared her throat, her cheeks heating. "I'm fine. What can I get you today?"

"Your famous coffee and bear claws again."

"Coming right up."

When she returned, and he paid for the order, he remained in place. She wasn't sure if she wanted him to leave or not. He unnerved her yet made her feel warm all over. She'd never had this strange reaction to any man before now, and she didn't know how to respond. It was scary.

"Can… I get you something else?" The words came out in a babbling stutter and embarrassed her further.

"I wanted to ask you a question."

"Okay." *Oh, God.* Was he going to ask her out? *Yes, yes, yes,* echoed in the back of her mind. As long it was in private, and he didn't try anything.

"Sheriff Grandy told me that Amy works for you and that she's been missing for a while. He said that you saw her a day or so before you got sick. Do you have any idea what she was going to tell you?"

The content of his question shocked Blake. Why would the sheriff confide in Henry about anything considering what happened the last time a journalist got wind of a story that could be damaging? Should she trust him if Grandy did?

She shook her head. "Not really, but she looked frightened."

"And she left when Gabriel showed up?"

"Yes."

He rubbed at his beard, one that was starting to grow on her. "See, something's off with this. When they brought you into the hospital, your pastor showed up.

When we were all waiting to hear something, I saw Amy down the hall, watching him. Something isn't right with those two."

"How do you mean?"

"I don't know yet. Simon asked me to do a story on Gabriel because of all his success with the church, but he immediately rebuffed the idea. Why wouldn't he want to toot his own horn? Get more people interested in your church? Get all the recognition he could? Wouldn't that be your goal if the rumors of a possible televised opportunity were in the air?"

Blake sighed. "Maybe he doesn't like talking about himself. Perhaps he isn't interested in that option, or could he have something to hide?"

He snapped his fingers. "The last one was what I was thinking. Was I wrong in assuming that you and Gabriel had a close relationship?"

She shook her head again. "I think he wants more than I'm willing to give. Friendship is all we'll ever share. Simple as that. Why don't you let me help you with this? I can get access to things you can't since I work for the church. Maybe I can find out something about him."

"No," he said, his eyes widening. "I don't know this guy. You could get hurt."

"He's not going to harm me." She touched Henry's forearm. "Please let me do something. Amy is dear to me. Like a little sister. If she's in trouble, I want to help."

He stared at her for a long moment, then sighed. "All right. I'll let you help, but you must promise me something first."

"What's that?"

"If you get a bad vibe from him or anyone else

working there, you have to back off."

"Okay. You have my word. Now, tell me what I should be looking for Wednesday night because I'll be at the church for services?"

"Anything that you can find on where Gabriel came from. There has to be some kind of paperwork on him somewhere. I know you're busy right now since you're reopening. How about we meet later today to work out a strategy?"

"Sure, okay." Blake's heart started that out-of-control journey again. Just the idea of spending time alone with him was exciting. "Why don't you come to my house for dinner? I don't think we should be seen out in public together. We don't want anyone getting the wrong idea."

He frowned and cleared his throat. "If you think that's best."

Blake knew right away he'd been offended by her suggestion. "Look, it's not you, Henry. I was upset when Gabriel managed to talk me into having a dinner with him two weeks ago. I don't want anyone talking. I had a bad experience in high school. People told lies about me, and Plain City has a grapevine that spreads from one end of town to the other. Everyone and their pets would know by tomorrow morning if we had a meal together in public. Can you understand why we can't do this out in the open?"

"I get it." He scribbled a number on a napkin and handed it to her. "Text me the details, and I'll see you tonight. I'll leave my car far away from your house."

"Okay, great. See you later."

Blake waited until he'd gone, then turned to find her mother staring at her, a mischievous grin playing on her lips.

"What?"

She shrugged. "Nothing really. Just that, the man is very handsome."

"Yeah, so what?"

"Just making an observation."

Blake slammed her hands on her hips. Her mother was up to something. But she wasn't going to speculate as to what. She didn't have time. Not only did she have a business to run, but now she had to figure out what she would make for dinner tonight.

****

Henry reached for the bottle of sparkling cider in the passenger seat and exited his car. He'd parked a block away and was nervous as hell, something he hadn't experienced with a woman since junior high. Blake Allen made him feel like an adolescent, something totally out of character for him.

He walked down the paved sidewalk and made his way to the front door, sucking in a calming breath as he rang the bell.

Footsteps nearing caused him more anxiety. The door came open, and Blake's appearance had him swallowing the lump that quickly stuck in his throat and almost made him choke. She wore a just-above-the-knee, flouncy dress, the color of a field of newly cut grass that almost matched her irises. The woman looked stunning.

"Come on in." She moved to allow him to step inside.

"How'd it go today? Was it busy?"

"So-so. We had a dozen or so people come in. It will pick up once they realize I've reopened."

"You didn't overdo it, did you?"

Jerri Drennen

"Right. Like my mother would let that happen."

Henry smiled. "Is she joining us for dinner?"

"No. Mom went out for a while. She's been hovering since I was released from the hospital. She planned to see a few of her friends since you were coming over. She thought I'd be all right for a few hours."

"I'm glad I could help. Something smells delicious. Oh, I brought cider." He handed it to her. Henry's mouth was as dry as dirt, and he wanted to crawl in a hole at how rushed the words came out. Anyone with half a brain could tell he was nervous.

He inhaled deeply.

After a moment of uncomfortable silence, she said, "Let's go to the kitchen. I made my mother's award-winning lasagna."

Henry followed her down the hall to the back where the kitchen was located, the aromatic smell getting stronger by the second, causing his stomach to growl. Better his stomach responding than his ardor since it was hard not to stare at her behind lightly outlined by her dress's material.

"Take a seat, and I'll get everything on the table."

Henry sat on the wooden chair, intent on looking at something other than Blake. She was such a distraction. Her home was clean—almost too clean—her deco sparse and he liked that. "How long have you known Pastor Gabriel?" he asked, hoping that asking questions would help keep his mind on the right track.

She carried a bowl filled with salad to the table. "Not long. Close to nine months now. He took over when Pastor Ames retired. I wasn't playing the organ at the time. Beverly Clearance was but she decided to step down a month or so ago. Strangely, she's been gone from Plain City for the past few weeks. Rumor has it, she's taking care of a family member in another state, but no one has heard from her."

Henry's stomach made a nosedive, fighting with whether to say something.

Nope. He couldn't tell her. He'd given Grandy his word and he wouldn't go back on it. Yet, this meant he had to talk Blake out of helping him. He had no idea if Gabriel had anything to do with this woman's death, but he wasn't willing to take that chance with Blake.

She carried a bubbling, cheesy concoction to the table, cut and placed a large slice onto his plate, then did the same on her own.

She sat and uncovered a bowl filled with rolls that smelled too good to pass up.

He reached for two.

She smiled, revealing the brightest teeth, a brilliant smile that stirred his body once again. There was something about this woman that set his libido on high alert, and yet he respected her too much to act on that desire. Something that was completely foreign to Henry.

He took a big bite of the lasagna and swallowed, his taste buds going wild.

"Is it okay?" Blake looked questioningly at him.

"Oh my God, it's amazing." He gobbled down another bite.

"My mother has won numerous blue ribbons for her recipe only my sister and I have."

"You have a sister?"

"I do. She lives in Little Rock with her husband and new baby girl. That's why my parents moved there—to be close to their new grandchild."

"Is she younger or older than you?"

"She's my baby sister."

"So, why aren't you married? You're beautiful, smart, and own your own business, not to mention the best cook in town. I mean, can we talk about those bear claws? I could eat them every day."

Her cheeks pinkened at the compliment. "Thanks. So, right after high school, I went to college and earned my degree and came back here and opened the coffee shop. My social life sort of took a backseat to building a successful business. I've been too busy to date, and guys don't like being second best."

Henry frowned. "I don't know about that. I have my career. I wouldn't begrudge my girlfriend or wife having a job she loved. I think you're just dating the wrong men."

She shifted on her chair. "You are probably right, but here in Plain City, that's what you get—that and everyone speculating on every encounter being a relationship. That's why I try not to go out with anyone for fear of the rumors that would arise. It's just easier not to date at all."

He shook his head. "So, it's like Peyton Place? Is that what you are telling me?"

"I guess you could say that. It's not all bad, though. You stay here long enough you'll see what I mean."

Henry doubted that. "I'm only here to get back on track, for the shortest amount of time. Given a chance, I want to go back to where I was three years ago. I'm a foreign correspondent. It's in my blood. Letting that go would be like cutting off one of my limbs."

Her beautiful eyes lost a little of their luster. She glanced down at her plate, then pushed her food around.

Why the change in her demeanor? Was it his confession of wanting to leave this town? Why would she care?

Maybe this was an excellent time to concentrate on his food. Or perhaps tell Blake not to get involved in this thing with Gabriel? "Look, Blake, I think you should stay out of trying to find something on the pastor. You have enough to deal with right now. You are just getting your strength back."

She stared at him for a long moment, then shrugged. "If you think so."

"Yeah, I think it's best." With that dealt with, he focused on his food. It wasn't every day he got a home-cooked meal with a beautiful woman—though he'd had two in the last two weeks. Maybe things were looking up for him.

Chapter Ten

Blake glanced over her shoulder, then stepped into the church's office a week later. She'd never done anything like this before, sneaking around Gabriel's domain to see if she could find something on where he'd been before coming to Plain City.

Henry didn't want her to do it, but she didn't care. At this point, she had to know if there was something the pastor was hiding.

And what was Amy's connection to him? Why would she worry her mother to death if something wasn't wrong? The whole thing made no sense.

With purpose, she slipped behind the desk and went for the drawer handle. It opened, and she quickly rifled through the contents inside. Nothing. She went for the next. Then the next. The middle drawer scraped while opening—loud enough that it sent her heart racing. She prayed that no one had heard. Inside was a small, black book and a gold ring with a cluster of rubies. Not a man's band. Blake had seen it somewhere before. But where?

Wait. Wasn't it Beverly's? Yes. She believed it was. So why did Gabriel have it? Maybe the older woman lost it when she was still working as the organist, and he'd found it on the church's floor. That was probably it. There would be no other reason for Gabriel to have the ring.

That figured out, Blake refocused her attention on

the book and picked it up as she heard footsteps down the hallway.

Oh, God. If she didn't hurry, she was going to get caught. It was time to leave.

Blake closed the drawer and stuffed the book in her pants' waist, then started for the door.

It opened, and Gabriel stepped inside, his eyes widened when he saw her. "What are you doing here?" he asked, staring intently at her.

"I was looking for that music we talked about." Blake was lucky she was able to reference that, otherwise she would have drawn a blank.

"Right." He walked over to a cabinet and opened the door. Inside were rows of folders. He pulled one out, then came back and handed it to her. "I think it's in here. I'd love you to play the piece on Sunday."

"I'll do my best. I'll run along now and see if I can't get started." Blake turned to leave yet was stopped when Gabriel stepped in front of her. "Look, Blake, I know you weren't happy with me for talking you into having a dinner after going to the print shop. Since that day, you've seemed so distant. Is there anything I could do or say to make up for that? I'm truly sorry if I've done something to upset you."

"No, no, everything is fine, really, Gabriel. It's just that I don't like mixing business with pleasure. I think it's best you know that."

He smiled, one she thought wasn't entirely true to form. "I will try to remember."

She nodded and raised the folder. "Okay. I better go and get started on learning this song. You have a good evening."

Blake rushed from the room. Gabriel caused a sense

of anxiety every time she was around him anymore. She wasn't sure if it was because of what Henry had told her or just a feeling she got, but either way, she was glad to be out of that office. It didn't help that she had his book stuffed in her waistband. It was like stealing—and from a man of God, no less. She hoped she wouldn't be struck by lightning on the way home.

She hurried down the aisle to the organ. She'd practice the piece a time or two, then go home.

Blake played each note and thought about her night with Henry days ago and how utterly disappointed she'd been when he told her how Plain City was not permanent—that he planned to leave as soon as he could. Being attracted to him meant nothing at this point. If he wasn't staying, then there was no reason to take their relationship any further. She and everyone in town were country hicks to him, and he couldn't wait to get out of *Deliverance*.

Blake ended the piece, sure she'd have no problem playing it on Sunday.

She grabbed her belongings, ready to go home to get some rest. Her business would keep her busy like it always had. Nothing else mattered.

As she pushed open the door to exit the church, a shadowy figure slipped behind her SUV.

Her heart took off at a painful rate. No way could she leave. Not when a person was lurking next to her vehicle. She needed to call someone. The sheriff? Blake reached into her purse for her phone and saw a missed call from Henry. She pressed to redial and waited. "Blake. I thought we—"

"Listen, Henry. I'm at the church. I think someone is waiting behind my car. Could you come and help me."

"I'll be there in ten minutes. Stay inside the building."

Blake ended the call and paced the floor, wondering what happened to Gabriel? Could he be the one hiding outside, or was he still in his office? She had no way to be sure.

If she trusted him more, she'd check, but right now, he made her about as uncomfortable as the shadowy figure out by her car.

Seconds ticked by as if it was hours until she heard tire squalling in the parking lot. She opened the door, relieved to see Henry getting out of his vehicle.

"Are you okay?" He rushed up the steps.

"Yeah, but someone slipped behind my car. I was just lucky to catch their shadow as they did."

"Stay here. I'll go check."

"No. I'm going with you." Blake was too scared to stay where she was. Besides, there was safety in numbers.

She followed closely behind him as they crossed the parking lot to her SUV. When they'd reached the driver's door, she breathed a sigh of relief. Whoever it was, was gone.

Henry turned to her. "Seems clear now. Are you sure you saw someone? Maybe it was the wind playing tricks with the trees."

"No. Someone was out here. Whoever it was probably took off when you showed up."

"You're upset." He touched her forearm. "Do you want me to give you a ride home? I could pick you up in the morning to come to get your car."

"Would you do that for me?" she asked, surprised.

"Of course."

She smiled. "Thanks. I'm shaken up and would appreciate a ride."

"Okay." He waved a hand. "Your chariot awaits." He led her to the passenger side door and opened it for her.

Inside, Blake took in a deep breath. Henry made her feel safe—something she'd never needed until now. This whole thing with Gabriel and Amy had her on edge, and until that moment, Blake had forgotten about the book she'd found in the pastor's desk. She leafed through her purse and came across the cell phone she'd picked up from Bev's yard. "Oh my gosh, I forgot I had this," she said more to herself than to Henry.

"What's that?" he asked, turning his head slightly to look at her, then back at the road.

"A cheap flip phone. It was next to the driveway at Beverly's. I thought maybe it fell out of her purse. That could be why she hasn't called anyone. I know I don't memorize numbers. I doubt many people do."

"Let me see if I can find out about it. I know who to call."

Blake handed him the phone. He probably did know all the ins and outs of just about everything since he was a reporter. She should also tell him about the book she had, but she wanted to first look inside.

"Here we are." He pulled up into her driveway. "What time should I pick you up in the morning to collect your car?"

"Is six too early?"

"Six it is. Now, I'll wait until you get inside, then leave."

Blake opened the door. "Thank you, Henry."

"I'm glad I could help."

She exited the car and hurried to unlock the door. Tonight was not what she'd expected. Never had she been too afraid to go to her car or simply walk to her house. All this seemed to happen in a short period of time. Hopefully, she'd get over it just as quickly because this feeling didn't sit well for her—not one bit.

****

Henry knew something wasn't right and couldn't find it in himself to leave. Not when that *something* could send this whole town into panic mode.

He glanced down at the phone Blake had given him and flipped it open. The damned thing was dead. He'd have to find a charger that would work for the old relic. If it was Beverly Clarence's cell, it could help the sheriff find who killed her. Everyone that knew the woman thought she'd left town to help a sick family member. If they only knew the truth. The connection with Gabriel just added to the need to find out more about the man. Why did Beverly step down from playing the organ for the church? Was it a difference of opinion? Or was it something else? Something that got her killed.

He leaned his head back on the headrest and blew out a breath. He planned to stay here all night. Beverly played the organ. So did Blake, and someone had been hovering around her SUV. Were they planning to do something to her? Could she be next to die? Henry wasn't taking any chances. She'd already been through enough.

He sat up straight. What if someone had already tried to harm Blake? They never did figure out what happened to her. What caused her illness? Maybe it'd been something sinister? And if that were the case, who was the common denominator? *Pastor Gabriel*

Jerri Drennen

Huntington.

Henry needed to find out who this guy was, and fast, before something else happened. But how? Gabriel probably wasn't even his real name. If he were living in a big city, he'd have numerous resources at his disposal. Here, Henry was going to have to dig up the man's past the old-fashioned way. Slow and tedious. But if it could save a life, he'd spend every waking moment doing it. The first chance he got, he'd need to interview several people at the church. That was a start and could lead to something.

But right now, he was going to concentrate on keeping Blake safe. Whoever was hiding behind her car was up to something—what, he could only imagine.

An hour passed, and he found himself dozing off.

He cupped his hands over his eyes, the sun blazing bright in the sky for the first time since he'd flown into Nigeria a month earlier. It had been raining day in and day out—he and Maverick, arriving on the tail end of the wet season—early summer, the humidity brutal. The two had traveled to the country to do an investigative piece on a militant group who'd indiscriminately killed hundreds and caused the displacement of thousands more, all in the name of ideology. He and Mav had been sloshing their way down the region, hoping to talk to anyone who'd come forward with information— everyone tight-lipped until last week when someone from the Nigerian consulate gave him a tip. "Make your way to Warri and meet up with Doctors without Borders. They were the eyes and ears on the ground and might be able to help shed some light on where to go next." It had taken them an extra day to get here because of the downpours.

"Who are we supposed to meet with?" Maverick asked, lugging his bag from the jeep.

"Bryan Claymore. He's chief security for the Doctor's."

Henry jumped from behind the wheel and glanced around the large, makeshift camp. "I say we find a shower and get a hot meal first. Then we'll go in search of the guy."

"Sounds good to me."

The two took a step toward the nearest tent, and a blast threw them back. Henry landed on his side, everything going numb. When the dust and smoke cleared, he saw Maverick face down in the dirt, blood gushing from his head. Henry dragged himself to his friend and tried to turn him over.

"Maverick! Mav! Mav!"

Henry woke with a start and looked around. The sun was starting to come up, and as he shifted in the seat, he found his hip ached. He shouldn't have slept in his car. It was too much for his damaged body. But he was worried about Blake. Then that damned dream. He was getting sick of reliving that horror repeatedly. Hell, he felt bad enough. He didn't need a constant reminder of how he'd gotten his best friend killed. All for a God-damned story. A setup, at that.

Why did *he* want to go back to that life? His sick obsession only managed to get the one person who understood his drive killed. You'd think that would have taught him something, made him rethink his career choices. There was no bringing Maverick back but losing him could be a learned lesson. That following a story, blindly, had consequences.

He stretched his arms over his head, catching a whiff

of himself. *Christ.* He didn't have time to go home and shower. Thank God he kept some deodorant and cologne in his console.

He popped the door open and reached in and grabbed the antiperspirant and dabbed it under his arms. Then he sloshed on a little aftershave. That should be enough to get Blake to her car. He'd then go home and shower.

He pried himself out of the seat and hobbled up to her door, then rang the bell and waited. She only took a few seconds to answer, looking too good for this time of the morning.

"Hi. Thanks again for last night."

Henry shrugged. "No problem. Are you ready to go?"

"Just let me grab my purse."

On the way to his car, she frowned.

"What?" he asked.

"Weren't you wearing that last night?" She pointed to his shirt.

Think fast, Kiel.

"You caught me," he said in a rush. "I haven't had time to do laundry this week."

She smiled. "Then I really appreciate you coming last night. I know you must be busy with the paper."

What was he going to say to that? Lying to her ate at his gut, but she didn't need to know the truth—at least, not yet.

He opened the passenger-side door, closing it once she was inside.

The drive was quiet—unnervingly so for him. When he pulled into the parking lot of the church, she turned to him. "I found this in the pastor's drawer in his office. I couldn't make any sense of it. Maybe you can." She handed him a black book.

"Does he know you have it?"

She sighed. "Gabriel might since he caught me in his office. I told him I was looking for sheet music. I'm not sure he believed me."

He huffed. "I told you not to mess with him, Blake."

"I know, but I wanted to see if he was hiding something. If what you said was true, and Amy was with him, I want to know what he's capable of. I mean, that girl is barely more than a child."

"I get that. I just wish the pastor hadn't caught you. Now, if he finds the book missing, you'll be the first who comes to mind."

"I know. But there's nothing I can do about that."

"I'll follow you to the coffee shop."

She shook her head. "You don't have to do that. I'll be fine."

"You're probably right, but I'm going to anyway."

"All right." She leaned in and gave him a light peck on the cheek, then opened the car door and walked to her own.

The simple touch of her lips caused the testosterone to surge in his body, a reaction that was foreign to him. Blake Allen was trouble, and yet, he, for whatever reason, relished it.

As she pulled out of the church's parking lot, he mirrored the action and followed, wearing a huge grin. That kiss was going to be the highlight of his day.

Get serious, Kiel. You can obsess over her later.

He had a phone, a book, and people to talk to now. Hopefully, one of those things could lead him to who Huntington was and if he had anything to do with

Beverly's heinous death.

At the coffee shop, Henry waited for Blake to get inside, then headed home to shower and change. That morning he'd go by Dean Miller Accounting and hope he could speak to the boss. He and Jenell were members of the Fellowship church. Maybe they could enlighten him about their pastor and what drew so many to the pews. That would be his reason for the visit, though he had an ulterior motive. Could there be something off about Gabriel? Was Henry the only one who'd noticed it, or were there others?

After a shower and a change of clothes, Henry was on the road again. He drove by the coffeehouse as Blake was flipping the closed sign to open. Henry would love to stop in and grab a cup of her famous coffee, but she distracted him too much. Maybe he'd stop in after he talked to Dean Miller.

Henry parked outside the accountant's office and went in, hoping that Jenell could finagle him an office visit with Mr. Miller.

He glanced around, not seeing her.

He cleared his throat, thinking she could be in one of the back offices.

Dean Miller stepped out and came toward Henry. "Can I help you?"

"I was hoping you'd have a few minutes to talk to me about your membership to the Fellowship church. Simon wants me to do a piece on the church's success since Pastor Gabriel has taken to the pulpit."

The tall man shrugged, looking almost annoyed with Henry. "What can I tell you? I don't know him that well."

"What do you think of your new pastor?"

"He seems like a good man. Better at giving a

sermon than Ames ever was. That's all I can tell you. Now, if you'll excuse me, I have a lot of work to do."

Henry knew a brush off when he'd heard one. Five minutes of the man's time was too long. His impression of the accountant, Dean Miller, had the personality of a stump.

"Thanks for your time."

Henry left the office, thinking that it had been a waste of time.

He had one member down, twenty or so to go.

Chapter Eleven

Days after her scare at the church, Blake walked into the Elks, surprised to see so many people were already there. Games didn't start for another half hour. She came early to get her Bingo cards and some popcorn and a good seat. Jenell was supposed to meet her but was running late again. Nothing new.

She stepped up to Gladys Reamer and paid for some cards, then went over and scooped out a bag of corn and started for the end table, Gabriel's presence making her step falter. What was *he* doing here again? Before last week, he'd never come. It was becoming a habit. He was looking right at her, his piercing stare sending a cold chill through her. Did he know she stole that book? Or was she just being paranoid?

"I need to talk to you," Jenell said from behind her, her usual bubbly voice sounding strained.

"Let's go sit down."

Once they were in their chairs, Blake studied her friend. "What's going on?"

"I was out early Thursday morning and saw you in Henry's car. Care to elaborate on why?"

"Oh, sure. I forgot to tell you I was leaving church Wednesday night, and someone was lurking next to my car. I was scared and called Henry. He came to help. I left my car in the parking lot, and he gave me a ride home, then picked me up in the morning to get it."

"Why didn't you call me? I didn't think you and Henry were on such friendly terms." Jenell's eyes narrowed.

Oh, God. Her best friend was upset. She could see that. Blake had forgotten that Jenell had her eye on Henry—yet another reason to steer clear of the man.

"I didn't want to scare you, too, Jenell. He simply helped me out. That's all."

"Where was Pastor Gabriel?"

"I don't know. I wasn't thinking clearly at the time." She didn't want to go into why she hadn't gone looking for Gabriel. Jenell would think she was silly. She probably already guessed that. Not that Blake didn't believe sometimes that about Jenell.

Her best friend touched her arm and stared at Blake intently. "Next time, call me. Don't worry about me being frightened. I'm not like that. I would have gladly come and got you."

"Okay. I get it, and I'm sorry I didn't call you instead." The last thing Blake wanted was to argue with her best friend or anyone else for that matter. Not now, not ever. She and Jenell were like sisters, and she didn't want that to change.

"I see the pastor is here tonight." Jenell tipped her head toward the man who was now standing in the corner, talking to Dean Miller. "What's up with that? I've barely seen him anywhere outside of the church."

Blake shrugged and set her cards in front of her. She hoped he'd leave soon so her jumpiness would ease up.

"Wow, the sheriff is even here tonight. Must be a special occasion."

Blake glanced around and saw Grandy next to the door, peering outside as if he were waiting for someone.

Her night was supposed to be nice and relaxing. So far though, it had gotten off to a bad start. "Oh my God, Henry's here." Jenell's exuberate voice returned. "I'm going to ask him to join us." Why did she have to do that? Blake wasn't sure if she could deal with him right now, too.

Her friend rose from her chair and shuffled sideways through the narrow path between the tables. Could tonight get any worse? Probably, but she wasn't going to think about that.

Jenell returned five minutes later with Henry in tow, her hand clutching his arm like he was her possession.

"Hello," he said, looking as uncomfortable as Blake with the situation. "How are you?"

Why did his eyes seem to warm when he looked at her? The gesture made her stomach flip flop. "You ladies are going to have to show me how to play this game. I've never done it before."

"Can you even believe that, Blake?" Jenell looked questioningly at her. "Who hasn't played bingo?"

Her friend seemed to be laying it on thick. Jenell wanted Henry, and he appeared annoyed by her, his rigid stance giving him away. His eyes connected with Blake's again, and she found that she couldn't look away. There was something about him that made her feel things she never had before. Unfortunately, her best friend was interested in Henry, and she'd never let a man come between the two. It didn't matter how handsome or drawn to him she was.

"B three," the announcer said, drawing Blake to her cards. *Just pretend he's not here and enjoy the night.* The first two games were a bust for her group.

"I need to speak to the sheriff. I'll be back," Henry

said, then got up and left.

"Could the man be any sexier? Look at that swagger?" Jenell ogled his retreating backside.

Blake refused to look. That would just make things more uncomfortable for her. "Incoming. Pastor to your left. We're surrounded by good-looking men tonight. How did we get so lucky?"

Blake didn't feel lucky. Gabriel might be handsome, but there was something dark lurking just under the surface of the man, and she would rather not be around him. Too bad there was no escaping this encounter—the next would be on her terms.

"Ladies." He took a seat next to Blake, much too close for her liking.

"Pastor," Jenell said when Blake remained silent.

She hoped that if she didn't say anything, he'd get the hint and leave.

"Can I speak to you alone?" he whispered next to her ear.

Blake's heart started to hammer in her chest. He knew about the book, and he planned to confront her with that fact.

"We're in the middle of a game." She knew it was rude, but she was too scared to face him right now.

"It won't take long."

She swallowed hard, then nodded and rose, following him toward the door. "Are we going outside?" she asked, hoping to get him to slow down.

He turned on her, his eyes black as coal. "I don't know why you'd steal something from me, Blake. What did I do to deserve that? All I've been is kind to you. I want my book back, and I want it now."

"I don't have it." Not a lie. She'd given it to Henry.

This time his dark eyes widened. "Where is it?"

"I'm not sure."

"I don't believe you." He grabbed her arm, digging his nails into the skin. "I think you know exactly where it is."

"Is there a problem here?" Sheriff Grandy stepped between them, forcing Gabriel to let her go. "Well," the sheriff prompted when no one said anything.

"Nope." Gabriel cleared his throat. "I was just leaving. I'll see you on Sunday, Blake."

She rubbed her arm, all the while wondering what, if anything, the pastor planned to do.

"Are you okay, Blake? Do you want to press charges?"

"No, of course not. I'm fine."

"You don't look fine. What was going on with you two?"

She swallowed a lump in her throat. "Nothing. Really. It's a church matter. Look, sheriff, I'm tired. I think I'll gather my things and go home."

He placed a hand on her shoulder. "Do you need a ride?"

"My car's outside, but thanks for asking. Good night." She turned and ran into Henry.

"Are you all right?"

"I'm feeling a little under the weather. I'm going to go home."

"Let me take you?"

"No," she snapped, then regretted it immediately. "Sorry. I have my car. I'm going to say goodnight to Jenell." She rushed to get her purse. "I'm going home. I'm not feeling well."

"What?" Jenell rose from her chair. "Did the pastor

upset you?"

"No, no, nothing like that. I think it's being back at work. I'm exhausted. I'll see you later." Blake wished she could tell her friend the truth, but she knew Jenell would be angry about her stealing Gabriel's book. It was just better to lie.

She rushed out the door, not bothering to look back, straight to her car. Inside, she locked the door and started the engine. She had no idea what Gabriel was going to do, but the whole experience made her more than nervous. She would need to watch her back from this night forward.

Blake pulled out of the Elks and drove down Main Street, bright headlights from behind, making her look in her side mirror. Was someone following her? Was it Pastor Gabriel?

She made the turn onto her street, her heart racing, praying the vehicle wouldn't make the same turn. Unfortunately, the car pulled up next to her driveway. She was terrified to get out of her SUV, afraid to even look behind her. A tap on her window had her jumping half out of her skin. "Are you okay, Blake?"

Relief engulfed her as she turned to see Henry leaning over, his eyes narrowed on her. He tried to open the door but found he couldn't. She quickly popped the locks and allowed him to help her from the car. "What's going on?"

Instead of answering, she wrapped her arms around him tight and held him. She needed comfort, and Henry had a way of making her feel safe and secure. "Where are your keys?"

"In the car."

"Let me get them. We'll go inside. I'll make you

some tea, and you can tell me what the hell happened."

Blake wasn't going to argue. Right now, having him here helped her sanity. That was all that mattered.

****

Henry placed the keys on the kitchen counter and glanced back at Blake. "Where do you keep your tea?"

"In the tin in the cabinet above the stove."

He rushed to put the kettle on, then opened the door and found the tin and set it on top the of island. "Cups?"

She pointed to another cabinet. Henry retrieved two mugs and placed them next to the tin.

"Now, tell me what upset you so much that you were shaking?"

"Gabriel asked about the book. He wanted it back and was a little forceful about it."

"Forceful how?" he asked, trying to keep his anger under control. If the pastor were here, he'd wring his neck.

"I'm okay. Gabriel just grabbed my arm."

Henry clenched his fists at his side. "So, what did you tell him about the book?"

"That I didn't have it. I don't think the pastor believed me."

The kettle started to whistle. Henry brought it over and filled both cups to the rim. He opened the tin and glanced inside, surprised it was loose-leaf. "Do you have a tea ball or two?"

She nodded, then retrieved something from a drawer and handed him the meshed orbs. He opened a ball and scooped up a teaspoon, a weird powdery substance catching his eye. "What kind of tea is this?"

"Earl Grey, why?"

"I've never seen a powder in tea before."

"Powder? What do you mean?" She stepped next to him and looked at the spoon. "No. I don't remember that being in there. What do you think it is?"

"I don't know, but we need to get this analyzed. Wait. The day you got sick, you said you had tea, right?"

"Yes, before I left for work, I had a few sips."

His jaw tightened. "This tea?"

"Yeah. I was in such a hurry that day. I made a cup. I don't think I even looked inside the tin and only had time to take a couple of sips before I had to leave, then dumped the rest down the sink."

"We need to have this tea checked. Something doesn't look right to me. I'll call Grandy. See if he can't come by."

Henry took out his phone and found the sheriff's number. No way was the man asleep. Not when he was still at the Elks when Henry left.

The phone rang three times before Grandy answered.

"What do you want, Kiel?"

"I'm over at Blake's and ran across something I'd like to show you. Do you think you could swing by and look?"

"If it'll get you off my back, sure. Give me twenty minutes."

He clicked end call and tucked the cellphone back into his jean pocket.

"So, what is it with you and Grandy?" Blake asked, studying him closely. "Every time I see you two together, you seem chummy, yet he talks to you like he hates your guts."

Henry couldn't tell her the truth, not until they found the killer. "Law enforcement and the press have always had a love/hate thing."

She stared at him, clearly doubting his answer.

"Okay. Well, now that you can't offer me tea, how about coffee instead?"

"That I can do." She quickly filled the coffeemaker with water and coffee.

"How did you end up in Plain City?" she asked while they waited for the coffee to brew.

"You want the truth or the version I tell everyone?"

She frowned. "The truth, of course."

"No one else was willing to take a chance on me, and it wasn't all about the rehab thing. I'm reckless. I don't think things through."

"How so?"

His loss was the last thing Henry wanted to talk about. It was so painful—much more so than the constant ache in his hip.

"It won't leave this room?"

"Of course not."

Henry wasn't prepared to talk about this. But he was going to anyway.

"I lost a close friend, and let's just say, I'm to blame for his death."

Her eyes widened.

He knew she'd react this way. Henry should never have told her. Everyone who knew what happened to Maverick looked at him with a discerning eye, and he couldn't blame them.

"How?"

Henry diverted his eyes. "We were on assignment in Nigeria. I was led to *Doctors without Borders* to speak with someone about a terrorist group I was doing a piece on. The day we arrived, a suicide bomber took out half the camp, along with my cameraman, Maverick. I fractured my hip and received a concussion. That's how I got hooked on painkillers." He glanced at her and was surprised by the warmth in her incredible eyes.

"It wasn't your fault, Henry. It was that bomber's. You need to stop blaming yourself."

"I wish it would have been me who died. My friend had a family."

Blake walked toward him, and his heart started on a steady spiral. He sucked in a breath when she squeezed his hand. "Everything that happens has a purpose. Your friend would have felt the same way had things been reversed."

He wanted to believe what she said to be correct, but it was hard getting over feeling guilty every day since the event.

Her hand left his and ran up his arm, sending a ripple of electricity through his body. He looked into her eyes and reflected there was something he'd never dreamed he'd see for him—passion.

At that moment, time stopped. Everything around Henry vanished, and all he focused on was Blake. Those amazing green eyes. Her full, lush lips—waiting for his.

He leaned in and was about to experience heaven on earth when the doorbell buzzed and caused her to jump away, her cheeks turning a sweet shade of pink.

Shit. Shit. Shit. Thanks, Grandy. Your timing's impeccable, as if you knew what was about to happen.

He headed for the door, opening it to find the sheriff, looking as annoyed as Henry felt about his timing.

"This better be good, Kiel. I was talking to Dean Miller at the Elks, and I didn't get to my point. Now, I'm going to have to stop by his office in morning to finish the inquiry."

"I'm sorry about that, but I need to show you something. It's important."

"All right. Lead the way."

Henry took Grandy to the kitchen, where Blake was standing by the sink, looking out the window. Was she afraid to look at him? Did she regret what just about happened?

"So, what's this I need to see?" Grandy's question drew Henry back to him.

"I want you to look inside that tin of tea and tell me what that powdery substance could be?"

"Powdery substance?" Grandy repeated stepping to the island and looking inside the rectangular container.

Using the spoon, the sheriff moved the content around, then scooped up some and drew it closer to look at and sniff. His eyebrows drew together, and then he looked at Henry. "This doesn't look right to me. I'll take the tin to someone I know locally that can have it analyzed."

"Blake had some the day she ended up in the hospital."

"But you haven't had any since?"

She shook her head. "I haven't."

"Okay. I'll have it checked, and I'll let you know what it is when I hear anything. You two have a nice evening."

"Yeah, right," Henry said, frowning. "Like that's going to happen now."

Chapter Twelve

To say that Blake couldn't concentrate on work today would have been an understatement. She'd arrived early, hoping to keep her mind off Henry, and, if the analysis on that powder had come back yet.

Because, what if it was tainted? Why would someone have done that? Who'd want her dead? And would she be so now had she drank more?

She'd gotten sick before she went snooping around Gabriel's office. Would that eliminate him?

Her mind raced a mile a minute on who it could be.

Then, to top everything else off, the avoided kiss with Henry had her nerves on edge. She'd wanted him to do it—knew the kiss would have been amazing, but Grandy's appearance squashed that, and she'd never know what it would've led to. *His tongue in her mouth. His teeth grazing her neck, onto her shoulder, down to the swells of her...Stop.* This wasn't helping her get anything done. She had the dough to knead, raise, and bake before she opened, or there'd be many disappointed customers this morning.

A knock at the back door made her jump. She quickly wiped her hands off on a towel and went to find out who was there. No one ever came by this early. Maybe it was Grandy? Or Henry. Both had her heart picking up speed.

Blake turned the knob and opened the door, shocked

to find Amy standing outside, tears pooling in the girl's eyes. "Oh my God, where have you been?"

Amy glanced behind her, her eyes darting left and right, sweat beading on her upper lip. "Can I come in?"

"Of course." Blake ushered her into the back. "Have you been home to see your mother? She's worried sick about you."

The girl's eyes widened. "No. I can't go home. I shouldn't even be here, but I had to come. You're in danger, Blake."

Blake took ahold of the girl's arms. "Why can't you go home, Amy? You're not making any sense."

Amy swallowed convulsively. "I can't tell you why. I just wanted to warn you to be careful. Please do this for me." She wrenched free from Blake and rushed out the door.

Blake wanted to go after her but knew she would refuse to say anything else.

Something was wrong. The girl was afraid for Blake, and she'd bet, her mother. It had to be why she wouldn't go home. She was scared that it'd put Deana's life at risk.

Blake had to call the sheriff. He needed to know what Amy told her. Maybe he'd be able to make sense of it all.

She sprinted to her purse, pulled out her cell phone, and pressed Grandy's private number he'd given her last night. He answered right away. "Are you all right, Blake?"

"Yes, but Amy came by to warn me again. She's in trouble, sheriff. She refuses to go home. I think she's afraid her mom would be in danger if she did."

"I'll call Deana when we hang up. See if she knows

anything. Oh, I had that doctor friend put a rush on that tea. He called me right before you did. It's Ricin, Blake. I need to know who had access to your house?"

Her mouth gaped. Someone tried to poison her. The confirmation about knocked her on her butt.

"Blake?" the sheriff asked. "Are you still there?"

"Yes. I'm just trying to take this in."

"Who has a key to your house?"

Blake rubbed at her temple. "No one that I know of."

"You don't have a hide-a-key somewhere, do you?"

"Yes. I do. I forgot all about that."

"Anyone else know about it?"

"No… Oh, wait. I sent Amy over one day to get something. She used the key to get into the house. Are you saying you think she poisoned my tea? No way. She just warned me to watch my back."

"Maybe she told someone, not realizing what she'd done until it was too late."

Blake's eyes clouded with tears. This was a nightmare. Would she ever wake up from it? Plain City used to be a wonderful, safe place to live. Now, she wasn't so sure.

"I want to send one of my officers over to keep an eye on you. Would you have a problem with that? In plain clothes, of course."

She wanted to say no but knew better than to do so. The sheriff would insist anyway. "All right. But he needs to stay inconspicuous."

"I'll tell him. Don't let anyone else in the café until he arrives."

Blake pressed end call and placed the phone on the counter. How had her life changed in a blink of an eye? One minute everything was moving along swimmingly.

125

The next, someone wanted her dead.

****

Henry turned the water to the shower on, not at all looking forward to spending another day trying to run Gabriel Huntington down to see if he'd agree to the article on his success. He just didn't have the patience for that. The man was avoiding his calls, and it was aggravating, to say the least.

He stepped inside the stall and was hit by cold water. "Son-of-a…."

He jumped back and grabbed his towel, wrapping it snugly around his waist. Where the hell was the water heater in this house? Probably in the lower level.

He padded through the narrow hallway to the back kitchen and found the door leading to the basement, flipping on the light on the way down. He ducked cobwebs, smelling mildew and another odor he couldn't place.

The water heater was in the middle of the room. As Henry walked toward it, a trail of red spots caught his attention. What the hell were they? Paint? He leaned down to get a better look.

Was it blood?

Henry followed the specks of brownish-red until he reached a wall panel. It was bizarre. He ran his hand over the seam where one panel met the next, a small nail sticking out as if it had been pulled away from the stud. Henry thumbed his finger behind the sheet and yanked, surprised that the wall gave way.

He glanced behind and saw thick plastic behind the panel. He pulled that free and got a whiff of something foul, something he knew wasn't right. Henry had to call Grandy and get him over here right away. He wasn't one hundred percent sure, but he'd bet the awards he had that it was something dead—someone dead.

He rushed up the steps and down the hall to his bedroom, grabbing his phone from the side table. As he punched in the sheriff's number, he slid into his underwear and pants, thinking he had to have been the only person in the basement since the death. You'd have to be blind not to see the blood.

"Grandy?" the sheriff said in a gruff voice, sounding out of breath.

"This is Henry. I need you to come over to my place. I think I found a body in the basement."

"A what?"

"A body," he said louder, zipping up his jeans.

"Oh, Jesus fucking Christ, Kiel. Did you bring the Grim Reaper with you when you came to town?"

What was Henry supposed to say to that? "I guess."

"Where are you staying?"

"One-Twelve Elm."

"Did you say one-twelve?"

"Yes. Do you need a hearing aid?" Henry shouldn't agitate the man, but in this case, it was just too easy.

"That's where Freemont lived when he was here."

"Does that mean…?"

"Don't touch anything. I'm on my way."

Henry tucked his phone in the back pocket of his jeans and reached for a shirt. He did seem to bring trouble. Then again, if Malcolm Freemont was in that wall, then he'd been here months before Henry came to town.

Twenty minutes later, he ushered the sheriff down to the basement.

"What brought you down here to begin with?"

Grandy asked once they'd hit the concrete floor.

"Cold water." Henry pointed to the heater, then to the red droplets on the ground. "That's when I saw these specks. I wasn't sure what it could be at first. I'm certain it's blood, and it led me to that wall panel. A few loose nails had me pulling at the sheet. It let go easily. There's a thick layer of plastic behind it. I didn't go any farther."

Grandy walked over, ducked his head behind the paneling, and then glanced back at Henry as he pulled a pair of latex gloves from his pocket. "Yep. This is a crime scene. I'm going to have to call the boys. Keeping this quiet is going to be impossible. I'd appreciate it if you wouldn't add to that."

"I won't say a word. It's in my best interest anyway since half the town would think I did it."

The sheriff smirked. "You're probably right. Can you find some other place to stay for a few days? You can't be here while we're processing the scene. Oh, and we'll need your prints to eliminate them from any we find. It has been quite the day so far today. First, Blake calls me to tell me Amy came to warn her to watch her back, then you and this. All in an hour of each other. It's going to be a crazy day."

Henry didn't hear anything Grandy said after hearing Blake was in danger. He had to go to her and keep her safe—something that shocked yet pleased him at the same time. He'd never been concerned about any woman before the blonde café owner—not even his mother. Maybe somehow this small town had changed him? Perhaps it made him realize that chasing a story wasn't the most crucial thing in life, at least not where Blake Allen was concerned.

Chapter Thirteen

Blake leaned down and upturned the stone where she'd hidden her spare key, snatched up the hide-a-key box and found her key inside. No one was going to get their hands on this again. She couldn't even imagine Amy telling anyone where it was, knowing that doing so could put Blake in harm's way. Then again, Amy did warn her of something imminent happening. Maybe she felt terrible about blabbing to someone. Could the girl have stolen her perfume?

She shook off the thought and glanced over her shoulder at the patrol car parked on the street. Roy Calhoun sat inside. It helped to know he'd be there all night, though being alone in the house had her on edge for the first time ever.

Blake waved to him, then walked to the front door and stepped into the house, immediately securing the locks. Yet another thing she'd never felt the need to do until now. That alone made her feel like a prisoner in her own home.

As she placed her stuff down on the entryway table, the doorbell rang, causing her heart rate to spike.

She forced a calming breath, then walked back to the door, checking through the peephole. Relief that it was Henry had her releasing the breath she hadn't realized she'd been holding. "What brings you here?" Blake didn't care. She was too excited to see him. He always made her feel safe, among other things—tingly feelings she didn't want to think about now.

He shrugged. "I have a favor to ask."

"What kind of favor?" She studied his face.

"I need a place to stay for a few days. I just got kicked out of my house."

"What? How did that happen?"

"Can I come in? If you have coffee, I'll explain everything over a cup."

She ushered him inside. "Let's go to the kitchen." Once there, she quickly made her way to the coffee maker and turned it on. "So, why did you get removed from your home?"

"Well, Grandy told me I have to find other accommodations for the next few days since the basement is now a crime scene."

Her eyes widened. "A what?"

"This has to stay between you and me, but there's a dead body in the wall of the basement, and if I had to wager a guess, I'd say it was the last reporter who had my job and who happened to live there before me."

Blake's hand flew to her mouth, and she sucked in a breath. Quiet, picturesque, Plain City had become *Twin Peaks* overnight. How had this happened? Why would anyone want Freemont dead? It made no sense.

With shaky hands, she poured two cups of coffee and handed Henry one. "I can't believe all this is happening. Amy tells me I'm in danger, then Grandy reveals that Ricin was in my tea. Can you believe that someone tried to poison me?"

"I had some idea that it could be that. I noticed the police cruiser outside. Will he be here all night?"

"Until he's relieved by another officer early in the

morning."

"Good. I want you to be safe, but I guess that means you won't want me hanging around."

Blake knew if he did, people would talk, yet she didn't care for the first time in many years. Henry made her feel secure, and right now, that's all that mattered.

"You're welcome to stay. I have a guest room upstairs. It has its own bathroom. I think we'll be okay." In the back of Blake's mind, she knew there would be innuendoes and that it might look bad to some people, but she'd deal with that later.

Maybe, while he was here, they could figure out who tried to poison her and why.

Wait a minute. Blake forgot about Jenell. If she learned that Henry was staying with Blake, she'd probably never forgive her.

She swallowed hard. "I'm suddenly having second thoughts about this, Henry. You must know that my best friend, Jenell, really likes you right? She might think something's going on with us."

He blew out a deep breath. "I get your point, Blake. But I'm going to be honest with you. I like Jenell. As a friend. You, on the other hand, I feel differently about. I'm attracted to you. If that's going to be a problem, then I'd better find another place to stay. I don't want to cause trouble. You've had enough of that."

Blake felt truly conflicted. Her best friend's feelings were important to her, yet so were Henry's. He was the first man she was drawn to. Even Billy, before his attack, hadn't elicited these strange sensations, so she didn't know what to do. "Okay. You can stay as long as you know, nothing is going to happen between us. I can't do that to Jenell. Is that something you can deal with?"

"Of course. I'd never try and force anything on you, Blake. Not ever. I get your concerns. I need a place to stay for a couple of days. Then, I'll be gone."

"Okay. Let me show you to the guest room."

****

Henry stepped out of the shower and grabbed a towel from the rack. Blake's guest suite was lovely, a bathroom connected. He wouldn't even have to see her if he didn't want to. Too bad his thoughts always meandered back to her and how she made him feel.

Henry understood her reluctance because of her best friend, and he'd need to be the one to fix that. He and Jenell would have to have a heart-to-heart. Henry knew he'd led her on, and he would have to fess up to that. Yet, right now, he alone had eyes for one woman, and that woman was Blake Allen. He just hoped Jenell would understand and not take it out on her. That might make Blake never want to speak to him again.

Once he dried his hair, he wrapped the towel around his waist and stepped out of the bathroom, a change of clothes laid out on the bed.

A muffled scream and a loud thump had him racing out the bedroom door and down the stairs, unsure of where Blake was in the house. He ran from room to room, his heart pounding wildly in his chest, panic setting in with every second that passed.

"Blake," he hollered.

Nothing. Not a sound.

He sprinted into the back entrance and skidded to a dead stop. Blake stood in the center of the room, a large, gray tote tipped over, the container's content scattered all over the floor. She was leaned over, picking something up. When she turned and saw him, her eyes widened.

"What happened?" he asked right before he realized he was only wearing a towel, and it was about to let go at his waist. He clamped his hand around the tuck, keeping it secured.

"I was looking for something, and a tote from above came crashing down on my head. Sorry I scared you."

Henry cleared his throat. "Are you okay?"

"I'm ah, fine." She refused to look at him, her cheeks flushed with color.

Hadn't she ever seen a man in a towel before? "You need help picking that up?"

"No. I can do it," Blake said in a rush.

"All right. I'll go back upstairs and get dressed." Henry could have sworn she looked relieved. Maybe she hadn't seen a half-naked man before—which meant she was a—no. No way could she be. Could she?

With that, he turned and headed out of the room. He was overthinking this. Blake had been surprised by his lack of attire—that was all it was.

Henry took the stairs and walked to the guest room. He'd get dressed, then offer to get them both some food. He was famished since he hadn't eaten all day.

While pulling on his pants, his phone rang. He glanced at who was calling, unsure of what to do when he saw that it was Jenell. Should he answer it? Tell her what was going on and hope she wouldn't go all *Crazy Ex-Girlfriend* on him. Not that they'd ever dated in his eyes. If in hers—only she knew.

He clicked accept. "Hey, you." He tried to sound casual.

"Are you okay?" she asked, alarm in her voice. "I saw four patrol cars parked outside your house. I was concerned that something happened."

"I'm fine. I'm glad you called. I needed to talk to you about this thing with us."

"What do you mean?"

Be honest and to the point. "I heard through the grapevine you thought maybe we were dating?"

"What? Who told you that?"

"It doesn't matter. I just wanted to get this cleared up. You need to know I'm not staying in Plain City long enough to be in any relationship. This is just a stop-off point for getting my career back on track." Henry's stomach clenched tight as the meaning of his words sank in. Why would it hurt to say goodbye to this tiny, hole in the wall town? Where there wasn't a damn thing to do besides writing silly fluff pieces during the day at a newspaper that only had a handful of subscribers or listen to tree frogs and crickets make an insufferable racket all night. Where was the fulfillment in that? Henry would be a fool to stay yet for some reason, the thought of leaving made his gut hurt.

"I understand what you're saying, Henry, but you still haven't answered my question." Jenell's words brought him out of his puzzling thoughts.

"What was that?"

"The patrol cars? Why are they there?"

"I'm not at liberty to say. You're going to need to ask the sheriff." Henry promised Grandy he'd keep the murder quiet, and he wasn't going to tell anyone besides Blake, no matter who asked. Everyone in town would know soon enough anyway.

Chapter Fourteen

Blake couldn't banish the image of Henry in a towel no matter how hard she tried. Yes, he was thin, but he was also all ridges and muscle, each well-defined, making him more appealing. From his belly button to where he'd held the towel together, hints of coarse, dark hair trailed down in a peppered line. She gulped at the thought of what it led to.

How was she going to deal with him staying, with that erotic picture in the back of her mind? She'd lose her sanity, and frankly, she needed all her senses to figure out who tried to poison her.

That fact alone still sent her to a dark place—had her wondering what she could have done to deserve such a horrible act. To her recollection, she couldn't think of one person in Plain City she'd hurt in any way, and Blake had always gone out of her way to help when she could. So, why did someone want her dead? It made no sense.

"Blake," Henry called, bringing her back to her first concern. *Sexy, towel man.* What was she going to do about him?

She might as well pull the scab off now. "I'm in the kitchen."

He entered the room, dressed this time. *Thank God.* Too bad she already knew what he looked like underneath those clothes. "I was going to get takeout. Any preference?"

The offer surprised Blake. It wasn't often that someone asked what she'd like. She always took a backseat to everyone else's desires. "Pizza sounds good. I think I have a coupon and a phone number for the Pizza Shack. I could call it in, and then you could pick it up."

"Sounds like a plan."

She walked over and opened a drawer to find the flyer that came in the Sunday paper the weekend before. "Is there anything you don't like on your pie?"

"I'm not a fan of anchovies."

Blake cringed. "I don't care for those either. I'll order a deluxe. It's got a little bit of everything on it."

He smiled and nodded. "That I can eat."

Once the pizza was ordered and they had a few minutes to wait, Blake leaned against the counter, unsure of what to do now. She couldn't allow her mind to wander again—not to Henry's half-naked body.

And there it is. Darn it!

"I have a question, Blake. Can you think of anyone who'd want you dead, or at least very sick?" Henry asked.

She mentally thanked him for the diversion. "I've been wondering that a lot since the sheriff told me about the tea. Amy had access to my house, but I know it wasn't her. I've been trying to figure out who she'd be willing to protect."

"Huntington," Henry said without hesitation. "I told you she was at the hospital when you were there. Those two have a strange connection, perhaps even a sexual relationship."

"Surely not. Amy's a child." The girl had never even talked to Blake about boys. How could this be possible?

"Hardly, Blake. Those girls are eighteen and

impressionable. Hell, I can even admit the man's got charisma. A young woman like Amy could've easily been manipulated into falling for him. Would be willing to do anything to make him happy. You, yourself, said the man has a way with words. Sweet talk can go a long way."

"Do you know that from experience?" she asked, studying his face closely.

He gave her a crooked grin, one that had her swallowing hard.

Dumb question. Henry Kiel knew exactly what to do since he had Blake completely mesmerized. Gabriel hadn't even gotten a second look.

"I'm no expert if that's what you're asking."

"Are you sure? I mean, Jenell liked you right away."

His grin grew into a mischievous smile. "What about you, Blake? Do you like me?"

"We weren't talking about me."

"We are now." He took a step closer.

The air in the room thinned, making it hard for Blake to breathe.

"I, ah, d…isn't it time for you to go get the pizza?" She slipped around him, moving toward the living room. "I'll find us a movie to watch while you're gone."

He sighed. "All right. I'll be back in twenty minutes, and please, no chick flicks."

She frowned. "What's wrong with a chick flick?"

"You got an hour?"

"Oh, just go get that pizza. I'll find something we can both agree on."

****

Henry woke to the blaring of his alarm. He planned to go to church with Blake. Time for him to find out what

137

all the fuss was about. There had to be a reason Huntington had grown his congregation by leaps and bounds. He wanted to watch Gabriel in his habitat, study him closely to see if he had a gift or if it was something else—perhaps darker and more sinister.

He rose and walked to the bathroom to turn on the shower. He was glad he'd brought a suit from home, though jeans were supposedly acceptable for the men. But not for the women of the church?

Wasn't that sexist?

He removed his underwear and got into the shower, adjusting the water to the perfect temperature. The shampoo Blake had on the bar was a bit fruity for his taste, but beggars couldn't be choosers.

He quickly washed his body and turned off the faucet. The simple fact that he'd be stuck in a room filled with people today had him on edge. Any closed in area that held dozens of people just reminded him of that day—one he'd like to forget—especially Maverick's death. In a day or two, it would be the anniversary date again. He always remembered it and tried to stay busy before, on, and directly after the date itself.

And now, with his mother being sick, not seeing her for so long only added to that guilt. What if she died without him saying goodbye? Could he go on living this isolated life and not feel like he was to blame for so much pain? Maybe living here in Plain City could help him focus on what was important.

He took in a cleansing breath and grabbed a towel to dry off, then stepped back into the bedroom. The alarm said he had fifteen minutes to get dressed and be ready to leave. *Breathe in. Breathe out.*

He and Blake were driving separately. They'd

discussed that the night before. Blake didn't want them spotted together, though, she agreed that him coming to church might be a good idea. Both he and Blake questioned Gabriel and were going to watch for anything out of the ordinary.

Henry quickly dressed, then walked down to the ground floor, where he found Blake standing in the foyer, dressed in a prim-and-proper green dress that matched her incredible eyes. She held a thermos mug out to him, her own matching one clasped in the other hand.

"I thought you could use a cup."

He smiled. "You know me too well." His comment made her cheeks turn pink, a blush that endeared her to him even more. She was a rare breed, and Henry found that intriguing on so many levels.

"I'll be sitting with Jenell toward the back," she said as she started for the door. "You are welcome to sit with us if you'd like."

"Thanks. I'll see when we get there."

Henry followed Blake to the church, then parked as close as he could to her SUV. The officer shadowing her had the hour off since Henry had offered to keep an eye on her. This gave the man time to go home, shower, and eat.

Henry allowed Blake to go in first, then headed for the door, taking in slow, even breaths. He could do this— one minute at a time. Sixty, if he could manage the complete service.

When he entered the building, an arm reached out and grabbed his. Henry turned to find the sheriff standing in the alcove.

"What are you doing here?" Henry asked, moving out of the path of the door in case there were other arrivals.

The sheriff shrugged. "Probably the same thing you are. I wanted to come and see what brings so many people here."

Henry had started to like Grandy. He was a smart man—more intelligent than he'd first thought. "How's the new crime scene coming along. Do we have an I.D. on the victim yet?"

"We're waiting on DNA from the man's only living relative—his grandmother who lives in a nursing home. The woman has dementia. That's how he'd gone missing for this long."

Henry wondered if he'd face the same fate. Yes, he had family, yet they barely spoke. Maybe it was time to change that.

"So, I heard you're staying with Blake. Jenell know about that?"

"No, and I'd like to keep it that way."

"She won't hear it from me. I don't need another murder in my town." He gave Henry a cockeyed grin.

"Where are you sitting?" Henry asked, hoping to find a seat in the last pew.

"Rear left. You can join me if you'd like, unless of course, you plan to sit between both your love interests."

Henry snorted, then gestured for the sheriff to lead the way.

The two stepped inside and took a seat. Henry looked around and spotted Blake and Jenell sitting together. Normally, she'd be in front playing the organ during the service, but since she'd taken that book from Gabriel's office, and he'd confronted her, she'd resigned. The pastor had replaced her with the wife of the man who owned the hardware store. Henry couldn't remember her name, but he did recall that she and her husband hadn't been particularly friendly to him when they'd met. Then again, he was a stranger, and held a job once filled by the dead man in his basement. He could understand that.

Chapter Fifteen

Blake glanced over her shoulder and saw Henry sitting with Sheriff Grandy. Could he be here for the same reason Henry came—to observe the pastor?

"Good morning, everyone," Gabriel said, drawing Blake around to the front of the church. "Today, I wanted to touch on something that we could all use in our daily lives—humility. False pride can get in the way of us doing things that might cause us discomfort. For example, someone being afraid to ask for help even if not doing so could cost them everything. Don't let your pride…"

Blake found herself zoning out to what Gabriel said. Instead, she studied the four women to her left who seemed enthralled, and then she caught movement from the door to the vestry, which stood slightly ajar. Gabriel must not have pulled it shut when he came to the pulpit. Movement from inside had her looking closer. A pair of eyes stared through the narrow gap—eyes she recognized right away. Amy's. This was proof that the girl was staying here at the church with Gabriel. Did that mean Henry was right—that the two were sexually involved while he was trying to date Blake? The thought sent a cold chill through her. Amy wasn't much more than a child. The idea itself made her lose any respect she had left for the man.

Her attention shifted to Gabriel, who was staring at

her—his eyes dark and menacing.

She swallowed a lump forming in her throat and looked down at her lap. The indifference she felt for the pastor last week had now turned to fear, a reaction that had sweat coating her back. Gabriel's eyes said it all. He despised her, and she'd need to stay as far away from him as she could.

Music started, and she stood, too upset to even look at the hymn book Jenell held out to her. Once the song was over, they all returned to their seats.

She refused to look at him again. She was too scared.

Minute after agonizing minute ticked by with her muscles tightening in her shoulders, causing them to cramp. The only thing she wanted to do was get out of that church and not come back—at least until Gabriel Huntington was gone.

"Blake, are you coming?" Jenell looked at her, confused.

"Yeah." She rose, grabbing her purse, clutching the strap to her side. She planned to breeze right past the pastor, not glancing his way. She didn't care how it looked to anyone. She would find Henry and go home and tell him what she'd learned.

"What's going on with you?" Jenell asked once they were out of the receiving line and down the steps. "You're not getting sick again, are you?"

Right here and now, she was going to lie again to her best friend, something she'd never intentionally done before this mess started. "Yeah, I'm not feeling well." Not a complete lie. The service had drained her. "You won't mind if I don't go to lunch at Connor's today, will you?"

"Of course not. Do you want me to come home with you?"

Should she tell her about Henry? *God.* Blake knew she should, but she also knew how her friend would react. It wouldn't be pretty.

She swallowed hard and shook her head. "No. I'm just going to crawl into bed and sleep. It's been a rough week back at work. I'll call you later."

"All right, but if you don't, I'll be calling you."

"Okay. I'll talk to you soon."

Blake raced to her car, noting that Henry had already left.

Once inside her SUV, she locked the doors and sucked in a deep, calming breath. This morning had started well enough, then turned into a nightmare.

She started the engine and eased out of the slot, spotting Gabriel in the rearview mirror headed her way. She wasn't going to stop. She planned to get the heck out of there.

On her way from the parking area, she glanced back again and saw the dark look on the pastor's face—only reaffirming she couldn't come back to Christian Fellowship church again. Not while *he* was here.

****

Henry watched Blake fly out of the parking lot and pulled away from the curb. He thought it best to move his car in case Jenell accompanied Blake to hers. He didn't want her thinking that what he'd told her last night didn't apply to her best friend.

He'd listened to Gabriel's sermon, unsure of why so many people found him uplifting, though, through his years in journalism, he'd learned how cult members were sucked in. They viewed things through biased eyes, were brainwashed into thinking their leader walked on water and could heal the sick and bring back the dead. He'd seen it overseas, with terrorist groups and their ideology. This was very similar.

Henry wasn't impressed—not one bit. When he noticed Blake's attention wandering, he observed her, and that's when he spotted the girl from the hospital peeking out the side door. It had to be where she was hiding. He'd signaled to the sheriff, who'd nodded that he'd seen her too.

Henry was the first to leave, Grandy right behind him. All the sheriff said once they'd exited was, he'd take care of it, that this was his job. Henry had to respect that.

Blake pulled into her driveway, and Henry parked on the street.

Her eyes widened when she spotted him as she was going up the sidewalk to the front door. She looked pale and was shaking.

Henry rushed to her side. "Are you okay?"

"I'm not going back there until Gabriel's gone. The look I got from him sent chills through me."

"Come on. Let's get you in the house. I'll make some coffee. We can talk." Henry clasped the keys in her hand to unlock the door and ushered her inside. He led her to the kitchen, forcing her to sit at the table, then went about making them some coffee.

"I saw Amy at the church." Her eyes clouded with tears. "That sick monster has somehow brainwashed the girl. Her mother needs to know where she is." She pulled her phone out of her purse.

"No, Blake. Grandy said he'd take care of this."

She swiped a tear off her cheek. "But shouldn't

Deana know her daughter is all right?"

"She'll know soon enough. Please just let the sheriff do his job."

Henry took two cups out of the cabinet, filled them with coffee, and carried both to the table. He placed one down in front of her, then sat, studying her features. The deep lines on her forehead and the pursing of her lips spoke volumes. Blake was angry and scared. That alone made him want to tear Gabriel apart. He was the reason for her anguish, and Henry hated to see her like this. "It's going to be okay, Blake." He reached for her hand and squeezed it tight. "Worrying is going to make you sick again."

She sipped her coffee and nodded. "You're right. It's just hard because Amy is almost like a younger sibling. The sisterly instinct in me wants to hurt Gabriel. How could *he* be so evil? He's supposed to be a man of God."

"Yes, but do we know that as fact? I couldn't find anything on the man."

Her eyes widened. "What? Nothing?"

"Nothing," he reaffirmed and took a swallow of his coffee. "At this point, I think that Gabriel Huntington isn't even his real name."

"How do we find out if that's the case?"

He smiled. "Perhaps by the picture I took of him while he wasn't looking. Don't worry. He didn't see me take it. He was too busy making eye contact with you and every other female in the room. I don't suppose you've noticed how many of your congregation are women? His draw has nothing to do with his riveting oration."

Her eyes widened further.

"You don't believe me? Come on, Blake. They're mediocre at best. His appeal is all about his looks and how he uses them." Henry knew he was right. He'd watched the women in the room. The pastor had them all seduced by his brooding good looks.

What they'd be willing to do for him was what Henry wanted to know. How far was Amy willing to go to win the pastor's adoration? Because she was clearly in love with Gabriel.

Would she poison Blake's tea to win his love in return? Would she murder for it? How about the woman in the barn? Could a teenage girl do something so heinous? What about the guy in the wall of his basement? Could she have accomplished that on her own? Or did she have help? Charles Manson didn't kill anyone, yet he was the catalyst to so many people's deaths. Was this what they had here? A cult member who would kill when told to?

That was the million-dollar question that could blow the roof off Plain City and uncover whatever went on inside those church doors when they were closed.

Chapter Sixteen

Blake woke to the sound of breaking glass. She jumped out of bed and raced toward the door, her heart pounding like a jackhammer in her chest. As she stepped out of her bedroom, Henry scrambled down the stairs. "Where'd it come from?" he asked, shooting past her to look around in the living room.

Blake followed, afraid to be left alone. Nothing looked out of the ordinary that she could see. They moved from room to room until they found shards of glass on the back entrance floor. An oblong object laid next to the shelving where the tote had fallen on her. The thing was wrapped in a white paper. She reached down to pick it up when Henry stopped her.

"We need to call Grandy. There may be viable prints on that thing."

Banging on the front door made Blake jump. "Who could that be?"

"My bet would be on officer Calhoun. Unless he slept through the racket."

The two walked to the front, Henry looking out the window first before opening the door. "It's him."

Henry allowed Roy in.

"Are you two all right?"

"Yes." Blake clasped her hands together to keep them from shaking.

"I heard a crash, then saw someone in the shadows

running away when I got out of the patrol car and streamed my light around the side of the house." He took in a breath. "Couldn't see who it was. It was too dark. I tried to catch them, but they disappeared into the backyard of the neighbor to your left. What happened?"

"They threw something through the back door window. We didn't touch it in case there were prints on it. It's something wrapped in paper. Do you have an evidence bag in your car?" Henry asked.

"I do. I'll run and get one. I need to also call the sheriff. Find out what he wants me to do. I don't want to leave you alone to run it back to the station if I don't have to."

"Don't worry about Blake." Henry placed an arm around her shoulder. "I can take care of her."

She sucked in a breath. Blake trusted that Henry could protect her. She didn't doubt that.

"I'll call the sheriff and see what he says. I'll be right back with that bag."

Henry tightened his hold on her. "It'll be all right. I'm not going to let any harm come to you."

Five minutes later, Roy came back, his light-blue eyes narrowed, deep lines burrowed around his mouth.

"What's wrong?" Blake asked, her stomach doing somersaults.

"It's probably nothing, but I couldn't get a hold of the sheriff. He's not answering his phone. I'll get the evidence," he said as he snapped on a latex glove. "Then I'll run back to the station. The sheriff might have left his cell phone on his desk. He sometimes does that when he wants to get some sleep."

Blake glanced at Henry who frowned. The officer didn't know what they did. *Please let him be okay.*

The officer rushed to get the object, then came back. "If you need me, call the station. They'll get me on my radio, and I'll come right back."

Henry saw the man out, then returned. "I have a bad feeling about the sheriff. I should have offered to help him."

"You know he would have declined any assistance. Let's not jump to conclusions yet. Maybe Roy was right, and he forgot his phone, or it's simply dead."

"Bad choice of words, Blake."

Henry's statement was spot-on. This situation couldn't be more dire. Grandy had gone to confront Huntington, and now he wouldn't answer his phone. Did that mean he was lying dead somewhere, or were they both letting their imaginations get the better of them? Blake prayed it was the latter.

"I'll go make some coffee." She headed for the kitchen. "It's going to be a long night."

"I'm going to run upstairs and get my phone and throw on a shirt. I'll try to call Grandy myself. Maybe he's trying to avoid the station, though, I really can't see him doing that."

Blake poured water into the coffeemaker, then added coffee and turned it on. She'd run to her room and slip into a robe. Thankfully, she'd been wearing a pair of her most modest pajamas when the calamity began.

When she exited her room, Henry was coming back down the steps. "I tried to call him. No answer. I don't feel good about this."

"Should we go try and find him?"

"Let's hold off for now. When Roy gets back, I'll tell him my concerns. Maybe they can send someone by Grandy's place to see if his car is there. Maybe he is just sleeping."

"You don't believe that do you?"

He shrugged. "I don't know, Blake, but I'm not taking you anywhere near Fellowship church. It's too dangerous."

Blake didn't want to go back either, yet if it meant the difference between Grandy living or dying, she'd go—in a heartbeat!

****

Henry would've gone to find Grandy if he didn't have Blake to worry about. He was angry with the older man for not calling in backup, if indeed he had confronted Huntington, a name he was sure now was an alias. Everyone had some internet history unless you were a *ghost*.

"Here." Blake handed him a mug of steaming coffee.

"Thanks." Henry took a sip, savoring the aroma. Since his sobriety, this was his drug of choice, and Blake made the best he'd ever had. Everything she did seemed to tower over anyone else. Best looking. Best baker. He'd bet she'd be the best kisser, too.

He blew out a breath. The last thing he needed to be thinking about was kissing Blake while she stood next to him, looking like a puritan in her pink and purple flannel pajamas and a bulky robe. Hardly sexy, yet somehow, she made it look good—too good.

He turned from her and walked to the window, glancing out at the motion detection light that for some reason had lit up, shining on the backyard like a set stage. With the hairs on the back of his neck charged, he scanned the lawn furniture, the fire pit, and the barbeque grill for a shadow or movement. Nothing, yet something triggered the light.

His heart came to a dead stop. The door in the back had its glass broken, which meant someone could reach in and unlock the lock.

He faced her again. "Blake, I want you to go to your room and lock the door."

Her eyes widened. "What? Why?"

"Just do what I say."

When she hesitated, Henry gave her a stern look. "Please, now."

She whipped around and left the kitchen.

Henry let out a strangled breath when he heard her door close and click. Maybe he was allowing his mind to conjure something that wasn't there, but it was better to err on the side of caution.

He placed his cup on the counter and crept to the back room, trying to remember if anything had been moved since the crash. He stood plastered to the doorway, watching for any movement. Seconds ticked into minutes. He noticed then that the pantry/entry had a door that you could lock. He quickly swung the door closed and secured the bolt lock in place. It would take a powerful man to get through it. That relieved him somewhat.

Still, was Gabriel watching them?

Henry grabbed his phone out of his jeans and punched in Grandy's number again. It rang and rang. *Shit. Where are you?*

A sick feeling radiated in the pit of Henry's stomach. He didn't want the sheriff hurt.

He turned to find Blake standing in the kitchen doorway. "Are you okay?"

"Yeah, but what if I wouldn't have been? You

shouldn't have come out until I told you to."

"I was worried about you. What's going on?" Tears filled her eyes, and Henry wanted to kick himself for scolding her. Sometimes he could be a real ass.

He walked over and pulled her into his arms. Those tears in her eyes were his fault. He needed to comfort her, no matter how uncomfortable it was for him.

The scent of her hair tickled his nose and stirred every nerve in his body. Hell, just being this close caused him to react. He pulled back, thinking it would be safer, only to be blindsided by the passion in her eyes. It wasn't smart under the circumstances, but he was going to kiss her.

He leaned in and touched her mouth tentatively, a light sweep across her full, bottom lip, testing her reaction.

When her arm slid up his chest and encircled his neck, Henry knew he was a goner. His mouth crushed hers, hard and hungry, her responsive moan only urging him on. He thrust his tongue out and delved into her sweetness, allowing a fire to take hold. Then, slowly, he backed her against the wall, his arms roaming over her waist, his fingers kneading into her skin.

Knocking at the front door had them both pulling back, Blake swallowing convulsively. "It's probably Roy."

Henry drew in a labored breath and stumbled down the hall to the entrance, trying to get his body under control. He was right. Blake was the best kisser, and he was sure if it had led to what they'd wanted it to, that would have been amazing as well.

He returned with Roy in tow, a grim look on the officer's face. "Did you find the sheriff?" she asked, knowing full well what he told her next wasn't going to be good.

"I went by the office and his house, and there was no sign of him anywhere. We'll keep looking, of course. Phil Tillerson will stay with you. He's out front now. I don't want you alone until this is over. Now, I better go. We've called in a few officers from Edmund to help in the search and we're meeting them at the courthouse. You two stay safe."

"Do you think something bad has happened to the sheriff?" she asked Henry once Roy was gone.

"I don't know, but I'm going to the church. That's where he was before he disappeared."

Her stomach clenched at the thought of him leaving. "Are you sure that's wise?"

"No, I can't say that it is, but I'm going to do it anyway."

Chapter Seventeen

Blake switched on the lights and went to the front of the shop to start some coffee. They'd all been up half the night. She was sure she'd have most of the force stopping in for some much-needed caffeine.

As she poured water into the first Bunn coffee machine, Phil's radio crackled, and a voice whispered something inaudible.

Blake froze.

Phil glanced at her; his face had lost some color.

"Was that the sheriff?" she asked, her whole body growing cold. If it was him, he sounded different. Weak and desperate.

"It was hard to tell. Try not to jump to conclusions."

That was never going to happen. If Gabriel had Grandy, he was in serious trouble. She was beginning to think the pastor was capable of anything since she assumed that he could have been the catalyst to her poisoning.

"If you need to go join in the search, I can stay here. I'll call Jenell to come be with me. I'm sure Dean would understand."

Phil shook his head. "Nope. My number one priority is to keep you safe. The sheriff would be the first to agree with that."

"I understand, but something's wrong. You can hear it in his voice."

"Look, Blake, we have six other officers and Kiel looking for him. I'm staying here."

Blake had no choice but to give in. All she could do was work and keep the officers supplied with coffee and donuts.

She stuck a filter into the coffeemaker, then poured in her coffee blend and turned it on. Then moved on to the next, and then the last. That completed, she headed back into the kitchen and started the prep work, rolling out the dough and sprinkling it with cinnamon and brown sugar, trying to concentrate on the job.

She couldn't help locate Sheriff Grandy, yet she could aid in officer morale.

Her cell phone rang, and her heart rate took off. Henry had promised to call if he found the sheriff. She grabbed her towel and wiped her hands as she raced for her phone. On the screen, it showed Jenell.

Her heart sank.

"Hello," she said, trying hard to keep her emotions in check. She couldn't let on that something was bothering her. Jenell was too quick to gauge her moods, and Blake wasn't allowed to tell anyone about Grandy's disappearance.

"I want to talk to you about Henry." Jenell's voice held a sharp edge that instantly put Blake on alert.

Great. This was the last thing Blake needed. Her best friend must have heard he was staying with her.

"Okay. What's up?" She didn't plan to say anything to dig her own proverbial grave, if indeed she was wrong.

"Are you having sex with him? Trisha Neal said she saw his car parked in front of your house early this morning."

Blake cringed. Trisha had been the one in high

school to spread lies about her and Billy sleeping together—a boy who just about ruined her life. It pissed Blake off that she went straight to Jenell with this.

"No, I'm not having sex with Henry." Blake dreaded what she did have to tell Jenell. "He is, however, staying at my house until he can go back to his own." Blake sucked in a breath, knowing that her confession wasn't going to go over well with her.

"Is this why Henry asked what I thought our relationship was the other night? Confessing to me that he wasn't staying in Plain City. Was this all about you, Blake?"

Blake's stomach clenched. She and Jenell had had their share of disagreements over the years but never anything like this. Over a man, no less. She could hear the pain in her best friend's voice. She knew she'd hurt her. "Henry told me the same thing, Jenell. He's not planning to stay here; this is just a drop-off point to get his career back on track. He wants to travel overseas again." Just saying this out loud had her stomach clenching tight. The last thing in the world she wanted was for him to leave.

Blake wanted to tell her everything that was going on, but she couldn't. Not until they found Grandy and got to the bottom of what Gabriel had done. If that meant the two would be at odds for a short time, then there wasn't a darn thing Blake could do about it.

"That's something you are going to have to ask him."

"I don't want to ask him. You are my best friend. What is going on?"

"I'm sorry. I wish I could tell you. I just can't right now."

"You can't or you won't?"

Blake's eyes filled with tears. "I have to work, Jenell. I need to go."

Right now, wasn't the time to deal with this. Blake was too worried, and Jenell was going to have to understand that, or not.

****

Henry had been sitting outside the church for two hours and hadn't seen or heard a damned thing. He was losing hope that Grandy was still alive. When he'd first gotten there, he'd banged on the church doors to no avail. He'd tried looking in the windows but saw nothing. Was anyone even inside? Maybe they'd taken the sheriff somewhere else.

But where?

The barn.

He started his car and pulled away from the church. It might be a wild goose chase, but what else could he do? Sit there all day, hoping to see something? At least this was being proactive. If nothing else, they could rule the place out.

The winding roads to the barn about made him sick, unlike when he'd been following the ambulance. He was nervously watching for the turnoff. By the time he found the gravel drive, his stomach was in knots.

He took the turn too fast and about hit a tree off to the side of the road. *Calm down, Kiel. Getting yourself killed isn't going to help Grandy.*

Henry blew out a breath and righted the car, taking the gravel drive slowly. If they were here, he didn't want to alert them to his presence. The barn was a hundred feet or so in the distance when he pulled over and killed the engine. It wouldn't be safe to drive any closer since his car was kicking up a cloud of dust. He'd go the rest of the way on foot.

He eased out of his car and clicked the door shut, then took off down the path. Every nerve in his body was on edge as he got closer.

Once the barn came into view, he ducked low and moved off to the side. He planned to go around the back again to listen before he looked in.

Around the rear of the structure, he inched his way to the window, his eyes and ears alert. A light moan sent his heart thudding loudly in his chest—so much so that he was afraid someone would hear.

He stood stock-still, listening.

Another groan of agony had him moving. Henry waited a moment at the window, afraid if he was spotted, it could get him and the sheriff killed.

He squatted below the window. There was no way he could have saved Maverick, but if Grandy was in that barn and alive, Henry sure as hell was going to do whatever he could to save him.

Another weak moan made him act. Things were getting serious. He had to do something now.

He rose slowly and peered into the window, not seeing anything until moving straw caught his eye.

He glanced around the barn, surprised not to see anyone. Could they have dumped the sheriff's body, thinking he was dead? Or was Gabriel planning to come back and finish him off? Either way, Henry had to get inside and see how dire the situation was.

He climbed in and slid over the sill. On the other side, he looked around again, then raced to the loose straw, pushing it away. Underneath, he found Grandy, blood oozing from his head, his breathing slow and shallow. So out of it that he didn't even acknowledge Henry. Not a good sign at all.

He reached for his cell phone, then cursed. He'd forgotten there was no goddamn cell service. Henry was going to have to drag the sheriff to his car and take him to the hospital himself. Better yet, he'd get his car and drive it up to the barn.

He shot outside and sprinted up the road. By the time he reached his car, he felt winded.

Henry jumped in and drove as close as he could get to the doors. Back inside, he went to Grandy. The man looked like death. He had to get him help. Quick.

Henry lugged him to his car, laid him in the back seat, and spun the vehicle around. He drove as fast as he could down the drive and onto the main road, his focus on keeping it between the ditches.

Close to town, he called 9-1-1 and relayed his location and where he was headed, hoping an ambulance could meet him along the way to the hospital. Grandy needed medical attention, and he needed it now.

Two miles on the other side of Plain City, he met the emergency vehicle. They quickly assessed the sheriff's vitals and transferred him.

Henry followed them to the hospital. Once he found out the sheriff's condition, he'd call Blake. He was sure she was a wreck at this point and Henry wanted to ease her mind when he could.

He had never been much for prayer in all his years, but right now Grandy needed divine intervention to survive, and he'd do anything and everything to make that happen.

Chapter Eighteen

Blake poured six paper cups full of her house blend and placed lids on top. Roy waited at the counter, having stopped in for a refill. He'd offered to take coffee to the rest of the officers in the area.

No sign of Grandy or his patrol car yet. That worried the heck out of her. Where could he be?

She placed the cups into a corrugated holder and turned around as the door came open.

Henry stepped inside, his eyes narrowed, his lips creased in a hard line.

Her stomach pitched and rolled like a small sailboat on an ocean storm swell. He was going to tell her something terrible—she knew it.

Before Blake dropped the coffee container, she set it down on the counter. "What's wrong?" she asked, preparing for the worst yet hoping for the best.

"He's alive, but that could change." He moved to take a seat at one of the tables near the counter.

"Where did you find him?" Roy's question was the one she'd planned to ask next.

Henry blew out a breath and leaned back in his chair. "The barn."

"Oh, shoot." Roy shook his head. "Why hadn't I thought of that?"

His statement confused Blake. "What barn?"

The men glanced at one another then her. "Just an

abandoned one out of town." Henry gave Roy a look that made him nod in agreement. The two knew something she didn't and wanted to keep it that way.

"What happened to the sheriff?" Blake would leave her inquiries about the barn for later. Grandy's condition was more critical.

"He took a hard blow to the head. He's in ICU. They had to put him in a medically induced coma to reduce swelling in his brain. It's a wait and see situation. The doctor said they'd know more in a few days."

"Is anyone there with him?"

"His ex-wife was called since she was his only contact reference. She looked shattered when she arrived at the hospital."

Roy nodded. "Those two have been on and off for five years now. As of a few weeks ago, they were on again. Millie will be devastated if he doesn't pull through," the officer said.

"I need to collect some things and bring them to her house later. I'll call some of the Fellowship ladies to bake some casseroles. We'll make sure she wants for nothing while he's recovering."

The first thing Blake would do was call Jenell. This was a time for them all to pull together. Jenell and her mother were the best at organizing stuff like this, and it would allow Blake and her to put their differences aside to help Millie.

She reached under the counter for her purse and found her phone, punching in her best friend's number.

It rang several times before she answered, "Yes?"

"I need you and your mom's help," she said, hoping that her friend wouldn't let their disagreement get in the way of helping a family in need. "The sheriff's in the hospital."

"What? How? I mean, what happened?"

"It's a long story, and I'll tell you later. We need to get everyone from the church to bring something by Millie's, so she won't have to cook for as long as the sheriff is in the hospital. I'll pull together a care package to take to the hospital. If you and your mom could take care of calling the ladies for casseroles or whatever else they'd like to make, I'd appreciate that."

"I'll get mom on it. She's so much better at that. Would it be all right if I come to the hospital with you? Dean closed again. He didn't even bother to let me know this time. I came in to find the closed sign in the window. I called to ask what was going on. He just said he had an emergency and wouldn't be open for the rest of the week. Weird in so many ways, but I'm free to go with you."

"I'd like that. Come by the coffee shop, and we'll go from here."

"I'll be there in fifteen."

Blake ended the call and glanced back at Roy and Henry. "I'll go get a basket and get some things together to take by the hospital."

She rushed to get a care package together, hoping Henry's presence wouldn't upset Jenell again. Her best friend had to understand that right now, she needed him to stay with her. He made her feel safe, and if Jenell knew about the Ricin poisoning, she'd want him there as well.

****

Henry stuffed his hands into his jacket pockets, his left hand connecting with something cold. He pulled out the object, taken aback that he'd completely forgotten about the cell phone Blake had given him.

He glanced behind him, relieved she was still in the

back.

"Roy, I need you to see if you can't find out if this is Beverly's phone and who called her in the days leading up to her death. I'm sure the charger is at her house somewhere. It was dead when Blake found it lying in her driveway. I'd forgotten she'd given it to me." That's when Henry also remembered the black book. It was at his house—one he still couldn't enter. *Dammit.* It wasn't like him to forget important things like this. Blake and his overwhelming attraction and concern for her had distracted him from doing his job right.

"I'll run it over to Fletcher," Roy said, drawing Henry back to him. "They have the technology to get into it and can get her phone and text records."

"I'd appreciate it if you keep me in the loop on this. I know Grandy and I didn't start on the best footing, but I like and respect the man. I want to know who did this to him."

Roy nodded. "I will. Thanks for having the sense to check the barn. He'd probably be dead now if you hadn't."

He handed the officer the phone and watched him pick up the tray of coffee and leave.

Henry took an emotional breath. He'd meant what he'd said about Grandy. The man was difficult on a good day, but Henry valued him more than most men. The sheriff had honor and integrity—a lot of people didn't.

He was glad there was an officer standing watch over him right now, too, since Grandy being alive would surface quickly in this small town. Whoever whacked him over the head would be worried that his identity would come out once the man woke up from his coma, *if he did.*

And, if that person was Gabriel, whom Henry would bet his career on, he'd love to be the one to bash him in the head as he'd done to the sheriff. He'd have zero remorse doing it. It was only what the ungodly guy deserved.

The door opened, and Jenell stepped inside, her easy-going expression changing when she saw him. She wasn't happy he was at the coffee shop, probably because Blake was here.

"Hello," she said in a matter-of-fact tone.

This was only going to get more uncomfortable if he didn't fix it now. "Hey, you. Why aren't you working?" He was going to ignore her coldness and hope it'd help to remind her of why the two were friendly.

She shrugged. "My boss closed up the shop again."

"Again?" he asked, just trying to make small talk.

"It's strange. *Miller Accounting* was always open, even on days it shouldn't have been, up until the last few weeks. I'm not sure what's going on with Dean."

"Could it be his health? You know men. They don't want to appear weak."

"It could be, I guess. I have noticed he's been kind of agitated lately."

Henry's interest piqued. "How do you mean?"

"I don't know, really. He seems on edge. Which isn't like him. Usually, he's laid back, almost boring."

"Did he tell you I stopped by the office a few days ago?"

She frowned. "No, Dean didn't."

Henry shrugged. Maybe he had forgotten or didn't think anything of the visit. All he remembered was the man's distraction—like Henry was a nuisance at the time. He'd seemed nervous that day? It was hard to say, yet Jenell's information intrigued Henry. A man, unburdened by life, all of a sudden acting strange and jumpy—a person who went to Gabriel's church. To Henry, this was a lead, one he planned to follow.

Blake stepped out from the kitchen, carrying a basket filled with baked goods.

This was Henry's chance to leave these two women to talk. He needed to sneak into his house to get that little black book, then do some digging into Dean Miller.

Hopefully, one of those two things could give him a direction to follow to find who killed Beverly and had unsuccessfully tried to do the same to the sheriff. Maybe, with any luck, by the end of the day, they'd have a murderer behind bars, and they could all go back to living their everyday lives again—not that his was ever really ordinary.

Chapter Nineteen

Blake released a calming breath and inserted her key into the lock of the front door. She was more than exhausted after getting less than an hour of sleep the night before. Worried about Grandy, then spending half the day at the hospital with Millie. With no change in the sheriff's condition—not unusual according to the nursing staff.

After five, she'd dropped Jenell off at her car across the street from the coffee shop, the two on good terms now, then she headed home without an officer in tow since Roy was in Fletcher. The other officers were out at *the barn* gathering evidence. Blake had no idea why Roy had left town, but he'd called a half-hour ago to say he'd come by her place soon to keep an eye on her.

She opened the door and stepped inside, immediately locking the deadbolt. She hated that she was frightened to be alone. Afraid of her shadow at this point, thanks to Gabriel. She would resent that for a long time.

Blake still couldn't understand why he'd tried to poison her. It had to be him. Though, she hadn't done anything to deserve something so horrible. Yes, she'd turned down his advances, but then again, he had Amy. Why would he even want to have a relationship with someone else?

The whole sordid thing was disgusting since Amy was so young. And he was a grown man. They shouldn't be together.

Her hands shook as she placed her purse and keys on the table in the foyer, then started down the hall.

She hadn't seen or heard from Henry since he'd slipped out while she was speaking to Jenell. He'd probably felt uncomfortable with the situation between them—especially since the tension had been about him.

She entered the kitchen and quickly made a pot of coffee, if for no other reason than to have some for Roy if he wanted a cup later.

Once it was brewing, the aromatic smell revived her as she leaned against the counter and took in a deep breath. The last few days had been awful, and she hoped she'd wake up soon from this crazy nightmare.

A knock on the back door made her jump. Why would anyone choose that entrance instead of the front? Unless it was one of her neighbors. Maybe Renee had seen her pull up and wanted to find out how the sheriff was doing.

Or maybe it was Henry.

She unlocked the door to her storage room and walked to the back, glass crunching under her feet. She was going to need to clean that up and replace the glass in the morning.

Her eyes widened when she saw Dean Miller standing on the other side of the door.

Blake quickly opened it, smiling at the man. "What brings you here?"

"I need you to come with me," he said, his look deadpan.

She frowned. "Why? What's going on?"

"Jenell got in an accident. I'll take you to her."

"What? When? I just left her a few minutes ago.

What happened?"

"She was hit on the way home. She's on her way to the hospital."

Tears filled Blake's eyes. Here, she and Jenell had managed to work out their problems, promised never to let anything come between them again, and now this.

She nodded and stepped outside, not bothering to grab her purse or lock the door behind her. All she could think about was getting to her best friend and praying that she'd be all right.

****

Henry ducked under the crime scene tape and unlocked the door, the seal breaking as he did. When he talked to Grandy again, he'd explain why he needed to get into the house. Hopefully, the man would understand—that's if he even recovered.

No, don't think like that. Grandy was a strong, healthy man, and he'll get through this.

Inside, he walked down the hall to his bedroom. The last time he'd seen the book was the night before finding the body in the basement, but he'd been too tired to look at it.

He rushed to the side of the bed and opened the nightstand drawer, reaching in to grab the book. He opened it to the first page, a name jumping out at him. *Bolton. What the hell.* Why would Gabriel have that name printed on the inside cover of the book? Could that be his real name? Gabriel Bolton? Did he own the property where the barn sat? It made sense. A dumping ground of sorts. Now he had a name—one to do some research on.

He turned the book's page, finding strange words and symbols and Roman numerals, then leafed through the rest of the book, finding similar things on each page. *Weird.*

Damn it all. What were the markings? What did they mean?

Where was his laptop? He needed to find out what it could be.

He glanced around the room but didn't see his bag. Where did he put it?

Crap. Henry'd left it at the newspaper. He needed to run down there and do some investigating.

He retraced his steps to the front door and left, tucking the tape back in place to make it look less obvious he'd been there.

It took him five minutes to get to the *Tribune*, noticing that the sun was starting to set. Blake was with Jenell, so he didn't need to worry about her.

He stepped inside the door and found he and the copy editor were the only ones there. *Good.* This way he wouldn't be bothered. The man barely looked at him, let alone asked any questions—only grunted a time or two at him during the weeks they'd worked together.

He booted up his computer on his desk and typed in the symbols and numerals in the book, a satanic ritual coming up. *Oh, dear God.* This was the last thing Henry expected.

What the hell was Gabriel doing? As he continued to read, his mouth slacked. It was a type of ceremony to gain power from the underworld. Bizarre and revolting since the man had to have sex with a virgin and then murder her after the act while people around him chanted and joined in.

"This is some sick shit." *Wait a minute.* Could this be why Gabriel had been interested in Blake besides the obvious—she was beautiful? Henry had seriously gotten *the virgin* vibe from her. Could the pastor have seen that, too? Again, thank God she was safe with Jenell right now.

Weird, Henry had been around the world and back, and this had to be the most egregious thing he'd ever seen. In a small, mid-western town, no less.

He shook his head, then typed in Gabriel Bolton, and a headline about a church in Southern Minnesota came up.

He clicked on the link and saw a picture of the remains of a black, gutted building, the date almost three years ago, the caption, *'Gatlin Fellowship Church burns to the ground with seven parishioners inside, including beloved pastor Gabriel Bolton.'* The picture was of Gabriel Huntington.

They'd assumed the man had died in the fire, but he was alive and well here in Plain City.

He needed to find Roy and let him know what he'd just found out. Had Gabriel killed those people to cover up his sick ritual and then burned the church to eliminate any co-conspirators and remaining evidence? Had he faked his death so he could move on to do it again to another unsuspecting town?

This was what Henry planned to find out before more people ended up dead at the hands of this sick fuck.

An idea hit him. Maybe he could see if there weren't similar church fires, with casualties.

He typed in fires that consumed churches, with deaths involved. Numerous links came up. It was going to take him some time to get through. Maybe narrowing the field by the pastor perishing in the fires would help.

This time six came up. Henry read through the first

one. Five people died with again their beloved pastor. No picture. In the second fire, seven perished with their new pastor. He scanned the last ones. More dead, always with the pastor. Always a different name. The other dead ranged from men in their fifties to young teen girls like Amy and Sara.

His phone rang, and he quickly answered it. "Henry, this is Roy. Is Blake with you?"

"No. She's with Jenell."

"Nope. I called her. She dropped her off at her car two hours ago. I went to Blake's house, and found the front door was locked. Back door wasn't. No sign of her. Strange, since her car's in the driveway, her purse and keys on the table in the hallway."

Henry's stomach lurched into his throat. The pictures of those burned-out churches flashed before him. "Go to Gabriel's church. I'll meet you there."

"What? Why?"

"Because I'd bet that's where he took her."

"But I don't think he killed Beverly. At least that wasn't who she last spoke with on her phone. A few text messages and the last call she received came from Dean Miller."

A man in his fifties. "Just trust me. Meet me at the church. I'll explain everything when you get there."

Henry shot out of the newspaper. If he didn't hurry, this time Gabriel would be killing someone Henry cared about—Blake. Then, he'd disappear again to start all over somewhere else.

Chapter Twenty

Blake shook as Dean shoved her into the back door to the church. Minutes into the car-ride with him, she'd realized he'd lied to her about Jenell having been hurt. He had no intention of taking her to the hospital. He was on a different mission, and he carried a weapon to prove that.

"What are you planning to do with me?" she asked once they'd entered the basement.

"You'll stay here until *he* decides." Dean took a key from this jacket pocket, locked the door they'd come through, and then walked to the other entrance leading upstairs.

"Why are you doing this? What did I ever do to you, Dean?"

"What you have done in his name, you have done to me."

Her mouth gaped. "What is that supposed to mean?"

"Gabriel is the father, the son, and the holy spirit. You have harmed My Father."

Blake stared at the man, wondering how he'd completely lost his mind.

"What have I done to Gabriel?"

"You stole something from him. Do you negate that?"

Great. How had Dean found out about the book? *Gabriel, of course.*

173

"Your lack of denial speaks volumes." With that, he turned and left, the click of the lock giving her no hope of getting out.

What was she going to do? She couldn't allow herself to panic. That wouldn't help her get out of this mess.

Maybe she could find something to get the door unlocked. Back in the day, she and Jenell had practiced picking locked doors at the school with bobby pins. Perhaps she could do the same here.

She glanced around, noticing a row of boxes on a shelf on the far side of the room. She rushed over to the shelving and grabbed one of the boxes, finding it filled with tithes envelopes.

"Darn it."

She threw it down on the ground and reached for the next. This one was filled with paper and retractable ballpoint pens. Maybe they could work.

She bent the clip up and raced to the door, inserting the tip into the hole and turning it left, then right. Her hands trembled and made it almost impossible to hang onto the implement. If she didn't get out of there and soon, she'd probably end up dead.

With determination, she turned the pen around in the lock, listening for a click. *Nothing.* Footsteps had her heart rate speeding up. Someone was coming.

She tucked the pen into her jeans pocket, stood, and walked to the middle of the room, grimacing when she spotted the boxes tossed on the floor. Maybe they wouldn't notice.

The door creaked open, and Gabriel stepped inside, his expression unreadable.

"Do you have my book, Blake?"

"I told you, I don't."

His eyes darkened to almost black. "Then who does because I want it back. I need it to finish what I started here in this town. I wish I'd never come here. Too many things have gone wrong this time."

"This time?" she asked, lost in what he was trying to say to her.

He stepped closer. "I thought there was something special about you, Blake. You were so kind and sweet when we first met. I thought you had a pure soul, were innocent of sin. Then that drug addict had to stick his nose into my business like the last news guy, and he upended my plans. So many things have gone wrong. I should have gotten out of here months ago."

Blake had no idea what he was talking about. It was gibberish.

"Where is my damned book?" he said in a frightening tone that sent Blake scrambling back toward the door.

"I gave it to someone."

"Who has it? Kiel?"

Blake didn't plan to throw Henry under the bus. She cared too much about him.

"Well," he prompted, moving toward her.

"No," she lied, wrapping her hands around her bare arms. Not only was the room cold, but Gabriel also chilled her to the bone. "I gave it to one of Grandy's officers. I don't remember which one."

His eyes widened and grew darker if that were even possible. "I'd get rid of you now, but I have other plans." He spun around and left, the door again getting locked behind him.

What had he meant by getting rid of her? Was he

going to kill her? What were those other plans? The mere thought terrified her and made her need to get out of there even more urgent.

She raced back to the back door and reached inside her pocket for the pen, forcing herself to focus on the lock. Her only hope was to escape and find Roy. Gabriel was evil—she saw that quite clearly in his eyes. She had no way of dealing with something like this since he had managed to convert a quiet, introverted man into believing he was the father, the son, and the holy spirit, and would do anything for him. *Like a cult.* Jim Jones and David Koresh or even like Charles Manson. To be able to convince others to commit atrocities in their name.

Could Amy have done something like that? Had she poisoned Blake's tea? Amy knew where the key was to her home. But if so, why warn her?

Second thoughts, maybe?

What had Dean done to protect his *God* besides getting her to the church? Who killed Malcolm Freemont? Could he have done such a thing? Or was that Gabriel's doing?

Enough. You need to get out of here before you find out the hard way how far they'll go to aid and abet a man using the pulpit in the access of evil.

****

Henry sprang from his car, ignoring the pain in his hip as he met Roy in the parking lot in front of the church. His body ached from lack of sleep and constant movement after an all-nighter and going most of the day today.

"Why do you think Blake's here?"

"I found out that Gabriel Huntington was Gabriel

Bolton in a small town in Minnesota and a handful of aliases in other communities across the mid-west. It's some satanic shit where he does rituals, sets churches on fire, and is assumed dead, along with a handful of his congregation."

Roy's mouth slackened. "You can't be serious?"

"I wish I was making this up. Why do you think the sheriff's in the hospital? This is bigger than we all could've imagined. This man is a serial killer, and if we don't stop him, he'll do it again, and frankly, I'd die before I let him harm Blake. Someone had already poisoned her."

"Should I call for backup?"

"Probably, but I'm not waiting for them to get here. Time is running out.

Henry charged toward the building. He planned to get into that church if he had to break down the door to do so. Blake was inside, and there was no way in hell he was letting Gabriel lay one hand on her. She meant too much to him.

That realization sent Henry's head spinning. He'd never felt this way about anyone before. He was *in love* with Blake Allen, and there wasn't a damned thing he could do about it now.

The door swung open, and he stepped inside, glancing over his shoulder to find Roy right behind him, his gun drawn. "You know how to use that?" Henry asked in a hushed tone.

"Sheriff wouldn't give me one if I didn't."

That made Henry feel a little better.

He moved down the church's aisle, looking left then right as he passed each row of pews. At the altar, he pointed toward the vestibule door.

Roy nodded, and they made their way toward the entrance. Blake was somewhere in this church, and Henry planned to tear the whole thing down to find her.

Chapter Twenty-One

Amy and Sara stepped into the basement. In Amy's hand was a white garment, Sara had a cup in hers. "I need you to put this on." Amy thrust it toward Blake. "And then you'll need to drink the liquid in this cup."

Tears filled Blake's eyes. This girl who'd worked with her for over two years, a teen Blake had helped so much, was now doing this to her. If she weren't living through it, she wouldn't believe Amy's betrayal. "What's going on, Amy? Why are you doing this?"

"Please, just put the thing on, Blake, or we'll be forced to do it for you."

The girl's threat sent Blake's heart racing in her chest. What was going to happen once she donned the garment? Should she refuse and fight tooth and nail to get out of the basement? Could she take both girls at once to escape?

No. Blake's best bet would be to pretend to go along and change into the outfit. Then, when the two led her to their destination, she'd attack.

She reached for the white robe and stripped out of her jeans and T-shirt and slipped the flowy gown over her head and smoothed it down. Whatever it was, it swallowed her up and dragged on the ground.

"I need your underwear." Sara picked up her discarded clothing.

Heat raced across Blake's face. "What? No. I'm not

giving them to you."

Sara grabbed her by the arm, her eyes glaring daggers into her. "Do it, Blake, or we'll rip them off you."

Blake's eyes widened. She couldn't believe the sweet girl she used to see in the coffee shop with her mother had become such a monster. All because of Gabriel. The man possessed some evil power.

"What are you planning to do with me?" Blake yanked her arm free.

"You'll find out soon enough." Amy still refused to look at her. *Coward.*

"Now, give up the underwear, and then drink this." Sara shoved the cup to her lips and forced her to drink it.

Blake choked on the horrible stuff, and unfortunately, she was going to have to give up her skivvies if she wanted out of the basement. That was her only way to get free.

Angrily, she tugged the silk bikini underwear off, picked them up, and handed them to the girl, giving her a heated glare. Then both girls shoved her toward the door, Blake almost losing her footing as she tripped over the gown's material. She caught hold of the doorframe before going down.

She turned her head and glared hard at Amy, who again looked away. She couldn't even face her. That alone terrified Blake. All she could do was bide her time and pray she had a chance to escape; otherwise, she'd probably go through unspeakable acts before her murder. Why else would she have to remove her underwear?

The whole thing brought her back to her senior year in high school on prom night. She and Jenell had gone stag, not that she hadn't had her share of offers. She

didn't have an interest in any of the boys who'd asked—
even Billy Cain, who she once thought was cute. But
she'd heard many rumors from too many girls who had
gone out with him. The boy couldn't take no as no. She
was surprised he wasn't in prison now. He sure as hell
should be. Hate would have been a kind word for what
she felt for him—a boy who'd cornered her, would've
raped her if not for the teacher who stepped outside. That
event had traumatized her to the point that she didn't
trust any guy—never wanted to be alone with one—until
Henry. She trusted him, was attracted to him, wasn't
afraid to let him touch her.

Did he know that she was in danger? *Please find me
like that teacher did, Henry, before it's too late.*

"Get moving," Sara said in a sharp tone.

Blake hadn't even realized she'd stopped as the
memory overtook her.

She lifted the hem of the gown and stepped through
the door, her eyes adjusting to the darkened hallway. The
lighting itself was going to make it harder for her to
escape. She hadn't been down in this part of the
basement before. So, she had no idea how to get out.
What direction to go. But she was going to have to try,
or she'd surely end up in dire straits if she didn't attempt
to escape.

A noise from ahead made her choice for her. She
clutched the gown tightly and took off running, the
footfall behind making her pick up speed. Blake wasn't
stopping unless someone made her.

****

Henry signaled to Roy that they were going in.
They'd stood in front of the door listening to the strange,
almost hypnotizing chant coming from inside, forced to

focus on the goal—freeing Blake if indeed she was there.

He turned the knob on the door and shoved it open. The sight in the room sent his stomach into his throat. The place was filled with people—all naked, all engaging in sexual acts. In all his years, Henry had never seen anything like it. The nights he'd spent with those sisters would be like a Christening compared to this sick depravity. Blake was on an altar, her hands and feet tied down. She wore a flowing, white robe. From the way her head lolled left and right, he'd say she'd been drugged.

Gabriel stood directly in front of her.

What the hell was he planning to do?

Images of Beverly's mangled body inundated him, causing his stomach to revolt. Just the idea of losing Blake threw him into a rage, a fury that he hadn't felt since learning he'd walked his best friend, Maverick, right into a trap and his death.

Gabriel turned from Blake and looked straight at Henry, his eyes as dark as pitch, smiling from ear-to-ear. "Just in time. I was wondering what was taking you so long."

Everyone in the room stopped their degeneracy and stared at him.

Henry swallowed hard and glanced around, recognizing a few people. The couple that owned the hardware store he'd met at the picnic, one of the waitresses from Connor's that had waited on him a time or two and, *what the hell? Jesus Fucking Christ.* Simon. His boss. The man who asked him to do the story about Gabriel in the first place. It didn't make any sense. Why ask Henry to do that when he was taking part in this? He had to know there would be the possibility of this coming out—of his exposure. Who was the woman he was with?

He didn't recognize her. No. Wait a minute. It was the snotty woman who'd been in Blake's coffee shop the first day he'd come in. The lady talking badly about him. *Hypocrite.*

"Give me my book," Gabriel said, walking toward him, drawing Henry's attention away from the odd couple.

Roy came out from behind him, his weapon aimed at the pastor's chest. "I want you to turn around and untie Blake now."

Gabriel continued to smile, his eyes dark as his soul.

Henry heard shuffling behind him, and Officer Tillerson whacked Roy over the head with his gun, the man going down. *Shit.* How many damned people were involved in this? Too many. Were there other people engaged in those other towns? Should some of them be behind bars? If he got out of this alive, this story was going to blow the roof off a lot of people's glasshouses. All for some sick pleasures.

The weapon used to bring down Roy was then shoved into Henry's back.

"Where is that book?" Gabriel started toward him again.

Henry's mind ran one scenario after another on how he could get Blake out of this without getting himself killed. Now, he wished he'd left the book at the office. *Wait.* Gabriel needed that book, which meant he planned to do the ritual. That also meant he needed a virgin.

Henry had an idea that might work. "I can give you the book, Huntington, or should I call you Bolton? Is there a sur-name you'd prefer?"

The man's eyes widened.

"Yes. I know what you've been up to."

"It doesn't matter." Gabriel gave Henry a shit-ass grin.

Henry wasn't going to let the man intimidate him. Not when his and Blake's life depended on him keeping a cool head.

"Like I was about to tell you, pastor. I can give you the book, and you can perform this so-called power ritual, but it won't work."

"Really? And why is that?"

He gave Gabriel that same grin. "Don't you need a virgin for this?"

"Blake's a virgin. I have that on good authority from a few of the women who know her."

"Yes, she was a virgin," Henry lied, hoping he was playing this right. "I've been spending the last few nights with her." He rubbed at his bearded jaw. "Not a virgin anymore."

Gabriel growled like an animal wounded. He might tear Henry from limb to limb, but at least he wouldn't rape Blake. Right now, she was all he cared about.

"Do you want me to shoot him?" Officer Tillerson asked, jabbing the gun into his left flank.

"No, Phil. I'll take care of him like I did the last news guy who stuck his nose into my business. Except, this one is personal. Blake was probably the last virgin in Plain City. God knows teenage girls no longer wait." Gabriel turned to Amy and Sara, who both blushed and tucked their chins to their chests. The pastor shook his head and turned back to Henry. "I'm going to enjoy killing you with my bare hands. You didn't deserve Blake. She was much too good for you."

Henry didn't give one shit what Gabriel Huntington thought of him. The man was a serial killer with a sick fucking fetish. If he had to die, he would at least get in a few good shots first. Without hesitation, he dived for the man, surprising him, knocking him off balance. The two went down on the floor, Henry socking Gabriel hard in the jaw, then gave him a left in the eye. The man returned the volley, a hard punch to the gut, so hard it about knocked the wind out of him.

Henry countered with a series of jabs to Huntington's middle, continuing until he turned on his side, trying to avoid his assault. Henry took a shot at his head again, striking him near the temple, stunning him.

Noise from behind Henry had him turning to see a dozen officers taking Tillerson down and rounding people up and cuffing them.

He rolled onto his back, relieved when they pulled Huntington up, and forced his arms behind his back and zip-tied his hands together.

Henry took in a breath, then rose. He needed to get to Blake. At the altar, he quickly untied her hands and helped her sit.

"Are you okay?"

"I'm not sure. Sara forced me to drink something."

"Let me take you to the hospital. I want you checked out." Henry was thankful that she didn't argue. There was no way of knowing what she'd been given, and he wanted to be sure she'd be okay. He loved her with all his heart, and she was all that mattered to him now.

Chapter Twenty-Two

Blake and Jenell sat down at the kitchen table, both having a hard time looking at the other. Blake had spent half the day at the hospital. They'd run tests since learning she had been poisoned. She was relieved to know that her health issues would not be permanent. That in time, she'd be her old self again—with energy to spare.

On the way home from the hospital, Blake had told her best friend everything—including the fact that she was in love with Henry. Jenell also knew her boss killed Beverly because she'd seen him having sex with Sara in the church basement, something that had shocked her friend to the core. The two had worked closely together for five and a half years. The realization had to hit Jenell hard, especially since she'd noticed a change in him after Bev's disappearance.

"What are you thinking?" Blake asked, fidgeting in her chair. The mere thought of losing her best friend devastated her. She knew Jenell had eyes for Henry, knew it'd be hard for them to move past this since friends didn't poach other friends' love interests. But Blake had to tell her the truth.

"Does he love you?"

Blake shrugged. "I don't know. It doesn't matter since he won't be staying in town anyway. You and I both know that was never in his plans."

Jenell reached across the table and squeezed Blake's hand. "Maybe if you tell him how you feel, he might change his mind."

"No. I can't do that. Even if Henry did feel the same, he'd come to resent me for holding him back. I love him too much to do that to him."

"That's nonsense," Blake's mother said, stepping into the room. "You need to tell him how you feel. I've been waiting for you to open your eyes and see that you needed more in your life than a business to run. Now that you've finally found love, you're planning to let it slip through your fingers. I didn't raise you to martyr yourself, Blake. You need to get your butt off that chair and go find him."

Blake shook her head. "I can't. I'm sorry but I want Henry to be happy and if that's without me then that's the way it has to be."

Her mother sighed. "I give up. Talk some sense into her, Jenell. She apparently won't listen to me."

"We'd better put on the coffee, then." Jenell rose and walked to the counter where the machine sat. "This could take all night."

"Coffee isn't going to change my mind, but I can drink a cup."

Jenell finished spooning coffee into the filter and turned it on, then came to sit down again. "I know how stubborn you can be, Blake. You also know how I've always been able to make you see reason. What if he feels like you do but doesn't think you love him? Men never want to look vulnerable. It's that testosterone inside them."

Blake contemplated what her best friend was saying. Jenell could be right, but then again, what if she wasn't?

What if she opened her heart to Henry and he didn't reciprocate her feelings? To her, that'd be much worse than not ever knowing the truth.

****

Henry sat down at his desk, booted up the computer, and opened a word document. He needed a byline—one that would grab everyone's attention. This story needed to be told and read by as many people as possible. There were others out in the country that needed to come forward with Gabriel's interaction, reveal who else might have been involved in the previous church fires that could be living their lives like nothing had happened.

The Complicacy of Blind Faith

By Henry Kiel

Plain City, Arkansas. A picturesque place that could have come straight out of a Norman Rockwell painting, where rumor runs rampant in the span of an hour, and everyone knows what you had for lunch. Yet, hidden in plain sight was a wickedness that spread like a virus throughout the community, infecting an editor, an accountant, owners of a hardware store, teenage girls looking for something beyond themselves, and shockingly, a member of law enforcement.

They found themselves drawn into a cult of sorts to fill a void in their lives. These were good, decent people, somehow seduced into thinking a man wearing a collar was the Lord God himself, and blindly followed him— undertaking unspeakable acts that would keep them entrenched in his grasp, even after realizing their errors. How easily a person of character can lose their way when a charismatic pastor lured them to the dark side.

I, for one, can see how easily it could happen. For years, I buried myself in my career until I'd lost everything in a manner of seconds in a bomb blast. That sent me to a place I never want to be again. We mortals are always looking for something to make us happy, fill that hole, and attain that elusive dream just beyond our reach. What we need to do is look around us, see the light in the darkness. Consider the small things that are easy to see if we truly look at the world. We need to find out where that emptiness starts and try to fill it with the things that bring us joy. A baby's laughter, songs that remind us of better days, anything that brings a smile to our faces.

Yet, with this unholy man, that hole was deep and limitless. He needed to control everything in his life, to achieve adoration, to use the church's pulpit to draw in the vulnerable and use them to amplify the dark impulses inside him—and once he'd done this in one town, he continued to prey on another, where the unimaginable didn't even register until it was already too late. That man was Gabriel Huntington here in Plain City, in Gatlin, Minnesota, he was Gabriel Bolton. If you've had an unexplained church fire with causalities that included the pastor or heard a rumor of one in another city near you, contact your local law enforcement. We need everyone's help to bring others who might have been involved in these horrendous acts to justice.

Henry ran the article through his editing software and sent it to their copy editor, who looked at him when his computer dinged, then nodded and went to work.

He leaned back in his chair and took in a breath. It'd been over a day since he'd left Blake at the hospital with her parents. He missed her terribly but wanted to give her time to sort out what had happened. She had a lot to deal with and didn't need him there to distract from that.

She was safe. Gabriel was in jail, along with everyone else who'd been in that room, including the two teenage girls.

Since their arrests, the police had learned a lot. Gabriel had murdered Malcolm because he'd learned what Henry had about his past. How Beverly had been killed in the barn by Dean Miller, and the events leading up to that. Two innocent people finding themselves in the wrong place at the wrong time. Sad in so many ways, not unlike his best friend Maverick. Lives cut short because of sick ideology.

Henry was done being angry. He was starting over with everyone who'd ever meant anything to him. The night before, he'd called his parents and found out that his mother was doing better. He planned to take a trip to see them in a week or two, and they'd seemed receptive to him coming. He wasn't going to allow his petty thoughts to get in the way of building a relationship with his family any longer, not now that he realized what it felt like to love unconditionally. Blake had become the air he breathed in and out, and he was going to tell her that in the morning when she went back to work. Until then, he was going to take it upon himself, since Simon was in jail, to oversee the next issue of the *Tribune*. That would take the rest of the afternoon and evening. Come hell or high water, the newspaper would be available in the morning for the paperboys and girls to deliver.

****

Blake washed her hands and dried them on her apron. She'd finished baking everything then loaded them into the display case. The clock read ten to eight. *Perfect timing.*

She replaced the dirty apron with a clean one and

stepped over to start all the coffeemakers, the smell of fresh brewing coffee reviving her senses.

Working would keep her sane—especially since hearing all the buzz about Henry's article in the paper that morning. It was a powerful piece, and she was sure he'd get recognition for it, that it would catapult his career into full gear. He'd get multiple offers, from large news outlets and he'd have his pick of cities to live in—away from her.

Emotion clogged her throat, and she swallowed hard, trying not to cry. This was going to be difficult, but she could get through it if she stayed busy.

She walked over and unlocked the door, turning the sign in the window to open, then returned to the counter and poured herself a cup of her house blend. As she brought the cup to her lips, the door opened, and Henry stepped inside. He smiled at her, and Blake just about lost control. She wanted to run. He was here to tell her he was leaving—that she'd never see him again.

"Can I help you?" she asked, her voice not giving away her turmoil.

He walked toward the counter, the smile wavering. He seemed nervous. Did he know how Blake felt? Was he afraid he'd hurt her?

"What do you suggest?" he asked, glancing up at the menu, then back at her.

Blake was instantly brought back to the first time she'd met Henry—his first visit to the coffee shop. She'd been so judgmental that day. Boy had things changed.

"Our house blend coffee is a best seller. The bear claws are to die for."

He scrubbed at his bearded chin. "Really? Is that strictly your opinion or everyone else's?"

"Both." She smiled at him.

"Okay. Give me one of each."

"Was that for here or to go?"

His lip twitched. "I thought I'd hang around a while if that's all right?"

"That's fine." Blake turned, her hands shaking as she retrieved the coffee and a bear claw. When she returned to the counter, she said, "I read your article in the paper."

"And what did you think?"

"I think it's good enough to get you out of Plain City and back to wherever you want to go."

His eyes widened. "Are you trying to get rid of me, Blake?"

"I just know that's been your goal all along, right?" Blake held her breath, knowing what was coming.

"Yes, that *was* my plan. But plans change. Town council offered me the editor and chief job at the *Tribune* last night and I accepted it this morning."

"Wait, what?" Blake had to have heard him wrong.

He took a sip of his coffee and set the cup back down. "I'm going to stay in Plain City and be the editor of the paper."

"But I thought…"

Henry came around the counter and stood right next to her. "I couldn't leave, Blake. Not when the one thing that means everything to me is here."

She looked up at him and swallowed the lump in her throat. "What's that?"

He shook his head. "Surely, you know."

"I, ah…"

Henry drew her to him, and he kissed her hard on the lips, then pulled back. "I'm not leaving town because you're here, and you have become my lifeline, my everything. I love you, Blake. I want to be with you forever."

Tears filled her eyes. Jenell had been right. If Henry hadn't come to tell her how he felt, she would have let him go and they'd both be miserable.

"Is your lack of response a good or bad thing?"

She sighed. "It's good. I love you too, Henry. I've never trusted anyone more, and I want to be with *you* forever."

"Okay. Good. Now, give me a quick kiss, and we'll finish this conversation tonight. I have a paper to run, and from what I see waiting at the door, you're going to have a busy day!"

A word about the author...

Jerri Drennen is an author of romantic suspense as well as paranormal and contemporary romance. Growing up on a farm in a tiny town in Minnesota was where she started reading romance and learned how to make up stories in her head. After meeting her husband, she moved to his hometown in Missouri where she now lives with one of their four children. Her kids call her the crazy cat lady.